THE FALL OF OPTIMUM HOUSE

ALSO BY ALICE ZOGG

The Lonesome Autocrat
Tracking Backward
Turn The Joker Around
Reaching Checkmate

THE FALL OF OPTIMUM HOUSE

By Alice Zogg

Aventine Press

This book is a work of fiction.

Published by Aventine Press
1023 4th Ave #204
San Diego CA, 92101
www.aventinepress.com

ISBN: 1-59330-503-6

Library of Congress Control Number: 2007937382
Library of Congress Cataloging-in-Publication Data
THE FALL OF OPTIMUM HOUSE/ Alice Zogg
Printed in the United States of America

To my daughters Franziska and Andrea

CREDITS

Many thanks to Charles Watry for suggesting that Huber could do with a sidekick. I followed his advice and created Andi. Credit is due to Valoise Douglas for sharing her bird-watching adventures as well as doing a superb job of editing. Joan Joe answered all the medical questions I had when researching this book. Thank you, Joan! I value Kelly Mobeck's assurance that the Barbie doll collection scenes I invented are credible. My daughter Franziska applied herself once more to the tedious task of proofreading another of my manuscripts. I could not imagine writing a book without her help. Again, Patricia Yankosky supplied the splendid artwork for the cover design. They get better and better with each book, Pat!

CAST OF CHARACTERS:

R.A. Huber
Private investigator; a woman sleuth par excellence

Peter Huber
R.A. Huber's husband; a writer

Antoinette LeJeune (Andi)
Huber's assistant; a dynamic young woman

Iris Camden
Huber's client; determined to find the person responsible for the transgressions at her facility

Jeffrey Camden
Iris's husband; a former football hero and now personal trainer at the gym of Optimum House

Emma Demitris
Modeling school principal; excels at her job

Kathleen Brackenbury
Academic teacher and tutor; decidedly British

Nadine Dugat
Dietitian; her knowledge in this field is undisputable

Cyrilla Washington
Modeling school student; lofty, graceful and proud

Nancy Zagarian
Modeling school student; her mother seems to see great promise in her

Susie Seales	Modeling school student; her expectations of becoming a model are slim, but she appears to enjoy the ride
Olivia Volmer	Modeling school student; seems preoccupied with the subject of sex
Roland Wempel	Health-program client; needs to lose some 50 more pounds
Paula Parsall	Health-program client; jolly, cheerful and loves to gossip
Troy Hesselman	Health-program client; the teen clearly resents being at Optimum House
Brant Ronnquist	Patron; a surgeon
Adam Applebee	Patron; an accomplished writer
Valencia Kirkland	Patron; an actress
Chad Richmond	Patron; CEO of a major corporation
Isandro Jimenez	Cook; manages to prepare food pleasing to the palate despite Ms. Dugat's directives
Dolores Garcia	Head housekeeper; rules her staff with an iron fist

Chapter 1

"Over there! I see the sign, R. A. *Huber, Private Detective*," Iris said, pointing at the ground-floor unit of a gray two-story office building. Her husband nodded and backed the silver Mercedes into a parking lot space. There was a noticeable limp in the man's gait as they walked toward the building.

Just before he reached to open the door for her, he asked, "Are you sure you want to go through with this?"

"Positive," she answered.

R. A. Huber, sitting at her desk, looked up as they entered. She perceived a couple in their late thirties. The woman was tall, blond and elegantly dressed in a forest-green suit with the skirt ending an inch above the knee. Her feet, extending from long legs, were clad in crocodile leather pumps. There was an aura of self-assurance and competence in her manner. By comparison, the man, although of above average height and broad build, seemed hesitant and almost shy in his demeanor. His round, boyish face was by no means handsome, but likable. They both looked familiar, but Huber could not place them for the moment.

Iris advanced into the room and took charge immediately, asking, "Mrs. Huber?"

"Yes. What can I do for you folks?"

"I'm Iris Camden, and this is my husband, Jeffrey Camden. We're here to hire you."

Huber got up to shake hands. Then she motioned Iris into the client chair, fetched a folding chair for Jeffrey and walked back to her own seat.

Iris watched the private eye's movements intently. What she saw was a trim woman in her early sixties. There was an athletic spring to her movements, yet she radiated elegance. She wore her salt-and-pepper hair in a becoming style pulled away from her brow. Iris detected only a minimum of makeup, discreetly applied. Her attire, a gray slinky pantsuit, was decidedly chic.

Looking straight into the woman's intelligent eyes, Iris stated, "I was hoping that you'd be overweight."

"Sorry to disappoint you!" Huber laughed.

Jeffrey gazed at the chessboard and chessmen on the desk and asked, "Are we interrupting? Looks like there's a game in progress."

"Oh, I always keep the chess set here. Every so often, like just before you came in, I play a solitary game to keep my mind agile."

She shoved the board and chessmen, including the captured pieces, to one end of the desk and said, "Now then, what do you want me to investigate?"

Iris began, "Things have happened at my - - I mean - - at our facility. At first I thought they were just practical jokes, but now I'm sure someone is out to ruin us and our business."

Huber asked, "What kind of business?"

"Have you heard of Optimum House?"

"The modeling school in the Big Bear area?"

"Yes, but it's more than that." She elaborated, "We started out with just a boarding school for modeling students. Then we added the health program for overweight people, and two years ago we built another new wing for patrons."

"I can picture the modeling school and the weight control program, but who are your patrons?"

"Let me explain," Iris said. "The school and health program are certainly worthwhile, but the enrollments have always been sporadic. The cost of keeping the place going is high, so when there was a slump, we had a hard time until the next boom. Then I thought of the 'patron' idea and it has worked out well." She turned to her spouse, "Didn't it, Jeffrey?"

He agreed, "Yes, Hon, one of your best brainstorms." And to Huber he added, "Iris has a wonderful head for business."

To which the latter remarked, "That might be true, but it's the modeling school that has always been my pride and joy."

The lady sleuth said, "I'm still in the dark as to who and what these patrons are."

Iris continued, "I was just getting to that. The patrons are famous persons or business people that have a need to escape from it all without being bothered in any way. They come mostly for relaxation, removed from their businesses, fans, stressful lives and so forth. They can stay in total solitude if they wish. Some even like to eat alone and have their meals delivered to their rooms. Others enjoy being pampered at the spa, getting facials, manicures/pedicures, et cetera. If they choose to socialize, we have a recreation hall where they can partake in anything from billiards and ping-pong to board games. We also strive to accommodate any special or extra wishes the patrons might have. Most importantly, we respect their privacy."

Huber said, "And I can imagine they don't mind paying a high price for that privacy?"

She smiled and replied smugly, "You've got that right."

"Okay, I'm getting a feel for the place." And looking from one to the other, she added, "I take it the business is a joint venture?"

Iris said, "Yes, I manage and oversee the entire operation, and Jeffrey - -"

He finished the sentence for her - - "is capable enough to help out with a little weight training."

Iris gave her husband a look and said, "Jeffrey is the personal trainer and in complete charge of the gym. The place could not function without him."

Huber commented, "Your establishment sounds like an enormous endeavor. You must employ a sizable staff."

"Actually, we manage with a minimum of employees. For the live-ins, there is Emma, my right hand where the modeling school is concerned. We have a teacher for conventional schooling. After all, most of our students are still in high school. Then there is a dietitian, a cook with his helpers, and Mrs. Garcia, who is the head housekeeper and has a flock of domestics under her wing. In addition, we have outside help who come in on a regular basis, such as a photographer, manicurist, beautician, makeup artist and masseuse. The gardener comes weekly to take care of the grounds and the putting green."

Astonished, Huber asked, "A golf course is part of your property?"

"Hardly! There's only a putting green."

"How long have you owned Optimum House?"

"Let me see - -"

Without a moment's hesitation, Jeffrey answered, "Nine years."

The detective remarked, "It must have taken quite a bit of capital to start such an enormous endeavor."

"Sure," Iris agreed, "but we both knew that our careers would be short-lived, so we saved up in order to start the business."

"Your careers?"

"Jeffrey was a football star, and I made good money as a model."

"I see." Then addressing the gentleman, Huber said, "Sorry, I should've recognized you, but I know nothing about football."

He smiled and replied, "I played professional football, quarterback to be exact, before I messed up my knee. I wouldn't have called myself a star."

His wife said, "Don't be so modest; you were a star!"

Huber turned to the woman and admitted "I should probably know about you too, but Iris Camden doesn't ring a bell."

"My maiden name was Westerholm."

"Iris Westerholm," Huber repeated. "Of course!" The image of a young couple featured in the L.A. Times over a decade ago came to her mind. Beneath the photograph she remembered the headline: *Football Hero to Wed Supermodel.*

Then she said, "Now that we have all that out of the way, tell me about the trouble at your place."

"People's belongings have been disappearing and later turning up in someone else's possession. Like I said, at first I thought someone was pulling pranks, but the latest theft is too serious to be ignored. A patron's valuable jewelry was stolen, and even though the bracelet was recovered a day later, the incident caused a lot of stress. We pride ourselves on the good name and reputation of our facility, and we especially make every effort to keep our patrons happy."

She sighed and continued, "Other nasty and spiteful things have happened recently. I am positive that someone is planning to ruin me. If word gets out that there is a thief running loose at Optimum House, enrollment will decline. Even worse, students, clients and patrons that we have currently attending might leave prematurely."

Her husband draped his arm over her shoulder and said, "Now Iris, I've told you before and I'm telling you again, you're taking this much too personally. I still think one of the kids, either from the modeling school or maybe the fat boy, is having a bit of a kleptomania problem."

"How do you explain the dolls, then?"

"Just spite and malice, I'm sure."

R.A. Huber put up her hand in a silencing gesture and said, "Okay, tell me each incident in detail and in chronological order, please."

Iris took charge again and said, "There might have been previous ones, but the first I was aware of would be the disappearance of Dr. Ronnquist's binoculars."

"When was that?"

"At the beginning of the spring school session, which was a month ago."

"From where were the binoculars taken, and if so, where did they turn up again?"

"He placed them on the chest at the dining-hall entrance before breakfast. When he was ready to leave for bird-watching, they had disappeared. Two days later, the cook found them tucked away in one of the kitchen cupboards."

"Please continue."

"Next, I think it was Emma's alarm clock. She overslept because the clock didn't go off one morning. In fact, it was missing altogether. She had set it as usual before going to bed. She assumed that one of the students was playing a practical joke, only she was not amused. I remember her being furious, canceling the class for that morning and ordering the students to sit around the conference table in silence facing one another until someone confessed. After three hours, she had to give up without result. The alarm clock was later discovered in one of the health-program client's rooms.

"Then the tutor's grading list was missing. I forgot if and where it eventually turned up again. I think one of the student's makeup case was also taken and later retrieved. One of the spiteful deeds was done to Cyrilla Washington, a student with a promising modeling career ahead of her. Her favorite outfit was lifted and a domestic found it in the wastebasket cut to shreds."

She paused and then went on, "I'm probably leaving some things out and they escape me at the moment. I've already mentioned the diamond bracelet. It belongs to Valencia Kirkland."

"The actress?"

She nodded.

"You said something about dolls. What was that about?"

"I have a Barbie doll collection. Some of the dolls are old and rare. I keep them displayed on shelves in the hallway. One day two dolls, a Barbie and Ken, were hanging from the swing with a string around each of their necks. You can imagine what that implied."

She shuddered and said, "I couldn't shake the horrible sight from my mind for days."

Huber remarked, "Although some of these acts are spiteful and mean, the thefts were relatively minor, except for the jewelry. Did you say it was a diamond bracelet?"

"Yes, worth a fortune."

"Are you sure it is the real thing? I'd assume that people, especially actresses, keep their real jewelry in the safe and wear a good replica."

"Not Valencia. She makes a point of only wearing real jewelry."

"But she has it insured?"

"Oh, definitely. When she first discovered the loss, she wanted to call the police right away. She needed a police report in order to file a claim to the insurance company. I pleaded with her to wait, and she gave me one day's grace. So I organized a search and we turned the place upside down."

"Where did you find it?"

"The thief had the nerve to hide it in my closet inside a shoe!"

No one spoke for a while. Then Iris burst out, "I've worked too hard at making the business a success. I can't bear to think we might lose it all!"

Jeffrey said, "Nonsense, we won't lose it."

Iris argued, "Even if our clientele should be loyal enough to overlook the thefts, the drowning cannot be kept secret. I only saw it mentioned in the local paper, and who, after all, reads the *Big Bear Grizzly*? But other media might have carried the story as well."

Perplexed, Huber asked, "Did someone drown?"

It was Jeffrey who answered, "Yes, one of the maids. It was an unfortunate accident."

"Oh?"

Iris said, "She apparently slipped and fell into the pool when scrubbing the diving board. I had no idea she didn't know how to swim. It certainly never occurred to me to ask people whether or not they could swim before hiring them."

Her husband must have realized what that sounded like to Huber's ear; how dare anyone drown in her pool! So he quickly softened her words by saying, "Don't blame yourself, Iris, you couldn't have known."

Huber asked, "When did the maid drown?"

"Last week."

"Was there an investigation?"

"Of course. The police concluded that it was an accidental death. There was no evidence of suicide or worse. Still, we can't afford for people to think that accidents happen at Optimum House."

The lady detective changed the subject, saying, "I'm sure there are private investigators available closer to your area. So how did you get to me?"

Iris replied, "Gina Timble highly recommended you."

"The name doesn't ring a bell."

"She was Gina Faracelli before her marriage. We know each other from our modeling days."

Huber exclaimed, "Gina, my dear Millie's daughter! So she is married to her doctor now. Are they still living on Catalina? How is she doing?"

Iris simply replied, "She's doing fine." Then she led the conversation back to her problems and asked, "Is there anything else you need to know?"

"You've put me pretty much in the picture, but just to satisfy my curiosity, I hope you won't mind answering a couple of questions."

"Sure, ask anything."

"Why did you choose the Big Bear area for the location of your enterprise?"

Jeffrey replied, "The answer is simple. My parents owned a weekend cabin with a stretch of land around it. Since we were looking for a secluded area, the location was perfect. We tore the cabin down and built the facility for the modeling school in its place."

"I see. I imagine the winter months are pretty gloomy, unless one is a skier."

"You're right, it gets cold and dreary. We close from mid-December until mid-March. The little business we'd get during those months wouldn't be worth keeping the place going." And with a smile he added, "Besides, closing up during that time gives Iris and me a chance to go on trips to warmer climates."

Then Huber glanced at the lady and said, "My second question is to you, Mrs. Camden. Do you guarantee a modeling career to the students?"

"Certainly not," she replied. "Out of a dozen students there might be two or three that will become successful models."

"Pardon me for being blunt, but isn't that getting their hopes up and taking their money for nothing?"

"Not at all. I'm up front with parents, or with students old enough to be on their own. At their consultation meeting before enrollment, I point out that there is no guarantee. The students generally enjoy the classes whether or not it leads to modeling jobs. After all, we teach them a great deal. We teach personal grooming, how to dress, proper posture, and show them how to walk, sit, stand and speak. We give them a good foundation for life. They graduate from Optimum House as young persons of poise, polish, class and breeding."

Huber raised an eyebrow and asked, "You can teach breeding?"

"Well, maybe not breeding, but at least good taste."

"How many people, besides the staff, do you currently house at your place?"

"Let me think. At the moment there are 18 modeling students enrolled, 16 female and two male. We have seven health-program clients and three patrons. Another patron is due to arrive in the next few days."

"So including the new patron, that makes 29."

Puzzled, Iris said, "Yes, but why the count?"

"I just wanted to get an idea of how large the facility is."

She volunteered, "We have 40 beds and can accommodate as many people. Not all of the students get their own room, though; some have to share with a roommate. The health-program clients always get their private room, and the patrons' accommodations are suites."

Then she said, "Now as to the plan. The sooner you come to Big Bear and find the person responsible for these antics, the better. We have to be discreet, however. I don't want an open investigation. Posing as a health-program client obviously won't do. Maybe you can come under the guise of a patron."

Huber grinned and said, "Now I understand your earlier remark about wishing I was overweight." And she continued, "If I decide to take on the job, I'll think of something."

"Why wouldn't you want the job?"

"I'm picky."

"Name your price, then."

"It's not a question of money. If a case interests me, I'll take it on. I shall think about it and let you know."

"How soon?"

"Give me a couple of days, Mrs. Camden."

There was nothing more for the Camdens to do but give their phone number and leave.

Chapter 2

Peter and Regula Huber sat at the kitchen table of their home in Merida, located in the San Fernando Valley at the foot of the Angeles National Forest Mountains. They had just consumed a dinner of salmon, boiled potatoes and spinach salad, and now lingered over coffee.

There was nothing remarkable about Peter's looks. He was of medium height and build, had a full head of white hair, a generous mustache and kind, hazel eyes. Hugging his cup with both hands, he surveyed his spouse. After 40 years of marriage he could predict her moods, thoughts and actions fairly accurately. Every so often, however, she surprised him with behavior totally out of character. That fact, he mused, kept their relationship interesting and alive.

He remarked, "You've been absent-minded all through the meal. Are you mulling over a new case?"

"Sort of," she replied. "I spoke with Gina Faracelli today."

"Millie's daughter?"

"Yes, only her name isn't Faracelli any longer."

"How is she?"

"She seems happily married to her doctor. We couldn't talk for long. I heard a baby in the background begging for attention."

"And?"

Regula did not respond and appeared to be daydreaming. Then she abruptly asked, "Does Optimum House sound familiar to you?"

Peter reflected before he replied, "I once noticed an ad in the paper about the place. If I'm not mistaken it's a fat farm near Big Bear Lake."

"You remember correctly, but that's not all. The business is divided into three segments: modeling school, weight control facility, and a fancy guest wing for the wealthy, the so-called patrons."

"What a bizarre set-up!"

"Sounds peculiar, I know, but the enterprise seems to work well, except for some recent agitations. Let me tell you the entire story." She gave a short version of the facts she had learned from the couple.

When she finished her narrative, her husband said, "I can't picture Jeffrey Camden as the owner of this strange outfit."

"Oh, of course! You must remember him from his football days."

"Yes, I do. He was a damned good quarterback in his prime. Then he got injured. I can't remember with what kind of injury, now."

Regula said, "He mentioned something about messing up his knee."

"Oh yeah, I think he ended up getting an artificial knee," Peter recalled. Then he asked, "Did you get the impression that his wife runs the business and that he's just along for the ride?"

"They assured me that it's a joint venture. Iris manages the place, and Jeffrey is in charge of the gym. However, I got the feeling that the lady has her heart and soul invested in the undertaking. I'm not sure that her husband does."

After a pause Peter asked, "What sort of a woman is Iris?"

"An extremely good businesswoman. To come up with this patron idea and make the whole enterprise work, and no doubt profitable, is ingenious."

"That's not what I asked."

"You want a more personal analysis?"

He nodded.

"She's tall and good-looking, of course. She wasn't a supermodel for nothing. Yet there's more to her than that. I'm certain she has a magnetism that influences most men and maybe some women."

"You mean she's got sex appeal?"

Regula smiled and said, "You'd be a better judge of that!" She continued, "That's not what I meant, though. There is something about Iris that goes beyond physical attraction. I can imagine that she is able to almost cast a spell on certain people."

"Were you affected?"

"No, but her husband was, and I'm sure most men would be."

"Interesting." Then Peter queried, "So what do you make of the thefts and the other misdeeds?"

"I don't know yet."

"And where does Gina fit in?"

"She doesn't. I just called her because she referred Iris Camden to me. Apparently they know one another from their modeling days. Since the woman didn't strike me as paranoid, yet seemed determined that someone was out to ruin her, I wanted Gina's input."

"So what did she say?"

"That Iris Camden was a level-headed person and if she felt someone was out to get her, it was probably true."

"Is that also your gut feeling?"

Regula carried their empty cups to the sink and rinsed each one before stacking them in the dishwasher. She finally answered, "I really don't know. Some of the transgressions are childish and tend to point to a student. But why would any student want to undermine the Camdens' business? Cutting the young woman's favorite outfit into shreds and the thing with the dolls is downright malicious. Jeffrey's suggestion that there is a kleptomaniac on the loose doesn't ring true either. As far as I know, people afflicted with that illness generally keep the stolen goods."

"Are you intrigued enough to take the case?"

"You bet!"

"That only leaves the question of how you'll get up there incognito." And he mockingly went on, "Posing as an aspiring model won't work, no offense, Regula, and neither will enrolling in the weight loss program. So you'll have to be a patron."

Regula said, "I doubt I'd fit in with that elite. No, Peter, it is time I made use of Andi."

"Who's Andi?"

"Antoinette LeJeune."

"And who is that?"

"I told you about the young woman who came to my office a few months ago, looking for a job."

"Oh yeah, the oddball. You're not seriously considering her, are you?"

"She'd be perfect for the job! I hope she's still available and hasn't started college yet."

Her spouse dubiously shook his head.

Chapter 3

On the drive to her office in Pasadena the following morning, R.A. Huber considered the prospect of asking Andi to come on board. Her encounter with the young woman had stayed vividly in her mind. One day in January, her office door had been flung open and Andi had blown in like a whirlwind. At first, the investigator was not sure of the young person's gender. All she could see was a lanky figure clad in jeans, a black leather jacket and cowboy boots. She could barely make out a face beneath the helmet. Then Andi had pulled off the headgear in a swift movement with both hands and vigorously shook her head, causing a cascade of wavy, auburn hair to fall around her shoulders. A pair of mischievous green eyes had peered at the investigator. It was now the beginning of May, but the dialogue that followed was imprinted in Huber's mind as if it had only been the day before.

The young woman had asked, "You the detective?"

"That's me."

"Miss Huber?"

"Mrs."

"Can you use any help around here?"

"Help?"

"An assistant, a right hand, a coolie, anything?"

Huber had smiled and asked, "What's your name?"

"Antoinette LeJeune, but I go by Andi. Only Daddy called me Antoinette."

"How old are you?"

"21."

"Try again."

"Okay, so I'm 18, but mature.   I'm also good at detecting."

"Did you graduate from high school?"

"Sure did; with honors too."

"You have a bit of an accent. Where are you from?"

Grinning, Andi had replied, "You too!"

"Fair enough! I'm originally from Switzerland."

"New Orleans, Louisiana, is my home."

"So you speak Cajun French?"

"Not much, but Daddy did."

"We'd better keep to English, then."

She shrugged. "You wouldn't get it anyhow.   It's pidgin French."

Then Huber had said, "Tell me a little about yourself."

"Like what?"

"Your family, your life, your interests, that sort of thing."

So she told her story. "I never knew my mother. She died when she gave birth to me. My daddy didn't remarry, so it was always just him and me. Daddy brought me up and took care of me. He didn't let me run wild, though. He made sure I was clean and proper, that I went to Church on Sundays, wore a dress at Christmas, Easter and on special occasions, and did my homework. He taught me stuff, and - -"

"What kind of stuff?"

"Oh, like how to play the fiddle and dance the Cajun Waltz, fishing, riding the Harley; loading, shooting and taking care of a gun. Oh, and cooking."

"Can you prepare gumbo and jambalaya?"

"Sure can." And winking, she had added, "I fix a mean jambalaya!"

At this point of Huber's musing, she thought it was significant that cooking came last on Andi's list of things her father had taught her. Being domestic did not seem the young woman's top priority, even if she fixed a "mean jambalaya."

Huber was driving east on the 210 Freeway and the Lake Avenue exit was coming up in two miles as she recalled the rest of the interview.

Andi had continued, "When I got old enough to date, Daddy made sure I wasn't running around with hoodlums."

"Is your father still living in New Orleans?"

"Daddy is dead."

"Not because of Hurricane Katrina?"

"He died last June of liver decease."

"I'm so sorry."

"No need to be. He had a wonderful life."

"How did *you* fare in the hurricane?"

"I was out of town before Katrina hit."

"Because you heeded the warning?"

"It had nothing to do with the hurricane. I was scouting colleges."

"I see. So you're in school now?"

She shook her head. Then she went on, "I came back to New Orleans in September, or to what was left of it. Then I sold Daddy's place and took care of his affairs. He owned a small bar in the French Quarter. There wasn't that much damage in that area since it's on higher ground. Daddy had life insurance and some savings put aside. He also paid into a college fund for me. I'm not touching the insurance money or the fund, but his savings and what I got for the property should tide me over for a while. Before he died, I promised Daddy I'd go to college."

"So how come you're not attending?"

"I promised I'd go, but didn't say when."

"I see."

Andi had continued, "So by end of October I was ready to roll. I shipped two suitcases with my stuff off to California, packed my essentials into the touring bag, hopped on my Harley and headed west."

"Just like that!" Huber had remarked, and then inquired, "Why California?"

"Got kinfolk here." And chuckling, she had added, "They're getting tired of me, I reckon. Been here since November. I'll move into a place of my own soon as I get me a job."

"How did you find my business?"

"Was in the neighborhood and saw the shingle out front."

"So you're a walk-in off the street, so to speak."

"I figured it never hurts to ask."

Huber had taken an instant liking to the young woman. So it was with regret that she had stated, "Sorry, there is no work for you at the moment. I'll keep you in mind, though."

Visibly disappointed, Andi had nodded and left her cell phone number with the private investigator.

Chapter 4

Regula could not remember where she had put Andi's number that day in January. Rummaging through the drawers of her desk and searching in the credenza proved fruitless. Then she checked the folders in the file cabinet. First she browsed through the A's, then L's, to no avail. Not ready to give up that easily, she scrutinized each folder, one by one. Finally! She found it under "M," for "miscellaneous."

She dialed the number and was about to hang up on the seventh ring when she heard Andi's Southern drawl on the line, "Hello - - stop that, Cleo!"

"Hi, Andi. R.A. Huber here. Am I interrupting something?"

"R.A. who?" she shouted.

"Huber. Is this a bad time to call?"

"Oh, Mrs. Huber! How you doin'?"

The detective could hear barking at the other end and asked, "Do you have a dog?"

"I've got four of them - - oh shit - - Duchess got away - - have to call you back," she yelled, and then the line went dead.

Regula laughed out loud. Four dogs and one got away! Andi was certainly full of surprises.

Some three hours later, the phone rang. Huber swallowed a bite from her lunch and picked up the receiver.

She heard Andi say, "Sorry I hung up on you. What a mess I got myself into!"

"What happened?"

"I walked the dogs along Beverly Drive like I always do, then - -"

"You own four dogs?"

"Of course not. I'm in the dog-walking business."

"Oh."

"When you called I was trying to squeeze the phone out of my back pocket. I must've let go of Duchess's leash for a second and she pulled herself loose. So we chased after her."

"Who is 'we'?"

"Me and the other dogs. Duchess is a Great Dane and some sprinter. At the corner of Wilshire and Beverly, she crossed over and almost got hit by a car. This spooked her, and she came to a stop in the middle of the intersection. We also left the sidewalk and raced into the street in pursuit, causing cars to hit the brakes and swerve. When Duchess saw us coming, she took off again and then sprinted away on the sidewalk along Wilshire Boulevard. I'd never have caught her if a man hadn't grabbed the end of her leash and handed her over. I am forever grateful to him. If I'd lost Duchess, her owner would've skinned me alive."

Huber could hear her take a breath before she continued, "Then I had to sweet-talk a cop out of writing me a ticket for jaywalking and causing a disturbance. I got away with just a warning. I think he wanted to get rid of us in a hurry as the dogs jumped up at him, trying to lick his face."

"Sounds like you had an eventful morning!"

"Sure did." Then she asked, "Why did you call?"

"To offer you a job, but I seem to be too late. You're in the dog-walking business."

Andi's excitement was evident as she blurted, "Detective work! You really wanna hire me?"

"On a trial basis, for now."

"When do I start?"

"What about the dogs?"

"I'm my own boss and have no stake in the business. After all, I just walk other people's pets. I can quit any time I want!"

"Good. Come to my office this afternoon and I'll explain the job."

Chapter 5

Andi burst into R.A. Huber's office with her usual vigor and plopped herself into the client chair. On the ride over she had told herself not to act like a kid in a candy store once she faced her prospective boss. Let Mrs. Huber do the talking, sit quietly, and just listen. However, as she now faced the woman, her good intentions were forgotten.

She leaned forward eagerly and said, "I'm tickled to death! When I dropped in on you that day and you told me that you'd keep me in mind, I was sure I'd never hear from you."

Huber smiled and said, "I appreciate your enthusiasm, but the case I'm planning to involve you in might not be to your liking." And she proceeded to tell her all she knew about Optimum House and the misdeeds that had taken place there.

Andi paid keen attention and then said, "So what do I do?"

"Enroll in the modeling school."

The young woman grimaced and said, "Pretending to be interested in becoming a model, but actually snooping around?"

"Exactly. Mr. and Mrs. Camden will know about you, but you'll have to fool everyone else. You'll have to be convincing. Can you handle it?"

Andi took her time before she replied, "I reckon, but I'm not good at all the girly stuff, like makeup and walking pretty in high heels." Then she grinned and said, "I guess I'll be learning all that in the school."

"That's the spirit!"

"You gonna be there too?"

"No, I'm not planning to, unless things get complicated. You'll be on your own."

"I won't disappoint you, Mrs. Huber."

"Let me make a few things clear. I want you to keep your eyes and ears open. First, get a feeling for the place and the people you're dealing with. You may ask questions, but make them in conversation. Never forget that you are planning to become a model. In other words, you'll have to live your role."

"So you want me to take on a persona and make up a background?"

Huber said, "No, no! Stick to your identity. If you invented one, you'd have to remember all the lies you'd tell and sooner or later give yourself away. You can stay true to where you're coming from and still live the role."

Andi nodded.

"If you discover anything, or if you have a gut feeling, under no circumstances are you to act on it. You'll report to me and I'll make the decisions. You need to be clear on that, otherwise I cannot hire you."

"Yes, ma'am."

"You also need to be on your guard. An investigator's work can be tedious, but at the same time there might be danger. So don't stick your neck out."

"I understand."

Then Huber asked, "Do you still live with your relatives?"

"I have a place of my own now. A one-bedroom apartment in Century City, with kitchen and all."

"Good for you! How much notice do you need to give your clients?"

"I have a backup person that can take my place."

"So what's the earliest you can be on your way to Big Bear?"

"Tomorrow!"

Huber smiled and said, "Today is Friday; let's make it Monday, then. I need to set you up with Iris Camden first. This will also give you the weekend to put your affairs at home in order and get ready for the trip."

"Do I bring a piece?"

"What piece?"

"I meant a pistol."

"You own a gun?"

"Daddy left me three. I sold the hunting rifle to a pawn shop; didn't think I'd do much hunting in California. I'm holding on to the Derringer and the Stinger pen pistol."

"Do you have a permit for them?"

"Daddy did. I reckon I inherited the permits."

Huber laughed and stated, "I don't think it works quite that way. You had best leave your pieces at home."

"Yes, ma'am."

"That's all for the moment. I'll call you after I've talked with Iris Camden."

No sooner had she stepped out of R.A. Huber's office and shut the door firmly behind her, than Andi took a leap into the air that would have made any dancer proud and shouted, "Yes, I'm a detective, yes indeed!"

Chapter 6

Optimum House was at the north shore of the lake; in other words, not at the well-known Big Bear Lake area near the south shore, or Big Bear City at the end of the lake, but the more remote area on the north side of it. The two-story structure had originally been built in the shape of a long, rectangular cube. Later, when the weight-loss program was added to the curriculum, extra housing for the clients was constructed, which made the building L-shaped. Then, more recently, the patron-wing was annexed on the opposite side, so that the entire structure now looked like an "E" without the middle line.

Despite the giant size of the place, the layout was simple. The ground floor of the main and original building consisted of the administrative office, kitchen, dining hall, conference room, classrooms and offices to one side of the hallway. Opposite were the library, Mr. and Mrs. Camden's suite, the gym, a pool with sauna and spa, and a recreation hall. The entire second floor was restricted to bed-and-bathrooms. At the moment most of the rooms were occupied by modeling school students, except for the three that accommodated the principal, tutor, and dietitian.

The west wing had six bedrooms with baths on both floors, designed to house a maximum of twelve health-program clients. The east wing contained six patron suites, three per floor. The main entrance was next to the parking lot at the original part of the building. There was a back entrance by the indoor pool and side entrances at each wing. At the north end of the parking lot, a separate, smaller building housed the domestic staff.

On Monday, Iris Camden was sitting at her desk in the administrative office. The room was large and, despite its obvious function as a place of business, was cleverly arranged to give an overall impression of warmth and coziness. The first thing people saw upon entering was a comfortable sofa group. The vase placed at the center of the mahogany coffee table was filled with a fresh bouquet of red tulips. Against one wall stood a curio cabinet displaying collectibles, and on the walls hung framed photos of past modeling school students who had become successful.

Iris stared at the computer screen in front of her. She was tending to the bookkeeping, but the figures were a blur. She had been at it for the last hour and could not concentrate. Her mind kept wandering to the problems she was facing. She looked beyond the screen and out the open window at the parking lot, without registering a thing. While absentmindedly fingering a castle-shaped paperweight, she thought, on top of it all, Chad is due to arrive any day now. Oh, Chad! Why can't you be reasonable? Of course she couldn't have refused having him as a patron, but they'd have to be extremely careful. Then R. A. Huber had called and informed her that an assistant would be handling the case. What a nerve! When she had talked with Gina, she had been under the impression that Mrs. Huber ran a one-person business. Gina had also assured her that the detective was discreet. Let's hope that applies to the young assistant too, Iris thought.

And then Jeffrey had been going through another spell of tossing and turning at night. Of course, he hadn't said a thing. He just liked to silently suffer, feeling sorry for himself and his handicap. Or was it more than that? Could he suspect?

Iris was snapped out of her reverie by the distinctive sound of a motorcycle racing into the parking lot.

Chapter 7

On that Monday morning in May, Andi was riding her Harley-Davidson in the diamond lane of the 405 Freeway, due north. She wondered why it was that a lone bike rider was allowed to use the car-pool lane, but hey, she told herself, I'm not complaining! Since her arrival in Los Angeles six months ago, she had first become familiar with the city of Pasadena and the surrounding areas while staying with her relatives. Then, when she had moved into her own apartment in Century City, she got to know the Westside pretty well, especially the Beverly Hills area where most of her dog-walking clientele lived. She had taken a trip to Disneyland, another to the L.A. Zoo, and several little outings to beaches in Orange County, but had never ventured out of the greater Los Angeles area. She counted her blessings and thought, lucky me! I get to be a private investigator and, as a bonus, ride the Harley into the mountains.

Mrs. Huber had warned her not to take the 10 Freeway even though it was the most direct route; the traffic through downtown would be a mess. Instead, she had said, "Drive through the Valley. Take the 405 to the 118 and then to the 210 East, which should prove more relaxing." Well, she mused, relaxed I am. After the fog, there'll be a bright and sunny day, and I'm off to a big adventure.

She was sure she could handle the assignment. So what if she had to participate in lots of girly stuff. She'd fake enthusiasm. It might even be fun, she decided. The important thing was not to give herself away. How had her boss put it? "Live the role."

About two hours into her ride the 210 Freeway led into the 30. She'd better pay attention now and start looking for the Waterman exit. A few miles farther, she spotted it, and there was even a road sign reading: *To mountain resorts.* She took the exit ramp and turned left on Waterman where the ascent into the San Bernardino National Forest began. The higher she climbed, the more exalted she became. The Harley performed well on the steep, winding road, and she leaned deep into every curve.

She stopped at one of the many turnouts to stretch and admire the view, getting off her bike and standing at the edge of the cliff looking down into the immense valley. "That can't be," she burst out aloud, "there ain't no ocean here!" At first glance it had seemed that she saw a vast body of water below, but then she realized that it was a huge layer of fog and haze and she was hovering way above it, basking in the sunshine.

Back on the road again, she passed the 173 turnoff to Lake Arrowhead and a sign that read *28 miles to Big Bear Lake.* Then she rode by the small towns of Running Springs and Arrowbear Lake while steadily gaining in altitude, riding the curvy road flanked by either pine trees or huge boulders. The Snow Valley ski area was deserted at that time of year, and soon after leaving it behind, Andi came upon the 7000-feet elevation mark.

At last she reached the fork in the roadway just before the lake. As instructed, she went to the left, which led to the north shore. Riding along the bank of Big Bear Lake she thought, damn, it is pretty up here! While passing through Fawnskin she thought, should be coming up soon now. About two miles farther she saw the sign-post *To Optimum House*, with an arrow pointing to the left. She turned into the curvy driveway edged by huge pine trees. When she came out of the last bend, the building came into view. She stopped the bike, planted her feet on the ground and took a good look. What a monstrosity! So this is where I'll be doing my sleuthing, she mused. I need to prove to R. A. Huber that I can do the job.

She suddenly lifted her face to the sky and said, "Hey Daddy! College is put on the back burner for a while. You understand?" Then she stepped on the gas pedal and rode the short distance to the parking lot.

Chapter 8

Andi shut down the motor, got off the motorcycle, and with a swift, forceful movement pulled the bike backward to make it rest on its stand. Then she removed the helmet and shook her abundant auburn hair loose. She tucked her headgear under one arm while grabbing the touring bag with her free hand and started to walk toward the building. Then she thought better of it, retraced her steps and went back to the Harley. She undid the straps to the second helmet attached to the bike and tied it to her touring bag. After all, there's a thief loose in this place, she told herself.

Iris watched Andi's process through her office window. Unconsciously, she made a quick professional evaluation: Passable height; long legs; naturally good posture; needs help with her walk - - lots of help! - - striking face. Mentally, she gave her overall verdict: Above average. But, good grief, a *motorcycle*! She shuddered.

Andi swung the office door open and entered with her typical gusto, saying, "Mrs. Camden?"

"Yes, and you must be Miss Antoinette LeJeune."

"Just Andi, please."

Iris inquired, "Where's the rest of your luggage?"

"This is it."

"Not much room for outfits and shoes, I gather, but you made up for it by bringing two helmets!"

The sarcasm was not lost on Andi, but she kept her temper and answered politely, "The bag is bigger than it looks; with the clothing rolled up there was room to spare." And without the slightest embarrassment she added, "I keep the second helmet for good luck."

Iris felt it was best to get to the business at hand and said, "Normally, I give a new student a brief summary of what to expect at the modeling school, and also what is required of her or him. In your case that is unnecessary. I'm sure Mrs. Huber gave you a briefing and you know what you are here for. I want the perpetrator caught as quickly as possible so that life at Optimum House can go on in an orderly and peaceful fashion again. I'd like to stress that you need to conduct the investigation in a discreet manner."

"Yes, ma'am."

"Do you have any questions about the facility in general or anything in particular?"

Andi said, "My boss explained your business to me, but I need to know more."

"Yes?"

"Please tell me what the job of each employee is, beginning with you, ma'am, if you don't mind."

"Surely," Iris said. "I tend to all the administrative work and do the hiring. I expect excellence from our staff and therefore pay them well. I manage and oversee the entire enterprise. The modeling school has always been my pet project, and I occasionally sit in on classes. If I see great promise in a student, I will refer her or him to an agent. As far as the health program goes, I counsel the clients and keep a record of their progress. I make sure that the patrons are comfortable and happy. If they have any extra wishes, I try to accommodate them."

"What kind of wishes?"

"If they're looking for a particular book or CD that we don't carry in our library, I'll order it. Or they might request certain food and drink that is not on our menu, and I'll make sure they'll get it. That sort of thing."

"Your husband is a personal trainer for the health-program clients, right?"

"Health-program clients are required to take the physical training, but students and patrons are welcome to participate as well. Everyone is invited to use the gym equipment as well as swimming in the pool and enjoying the spa and sauna."

Andi nodded.

Iris continued, "As far as the rest of the workforce goes, Emma Demitris is the principal of the modeling school. She's in charge of the students and teaches the classes. Occasionally, she'll ask me to give her a hand, but she is more than capable of handling the job on her own."

"Is she also a former model?"

"Yes, I know her from our modeling days. She and I go back a long way." And she continued, "Kathleen Brackenbury teaches academics. Her job is self-explanatory. Then there's Nadine Dugat, our dietitian. Her function is also evident."

Andi said, "She calculates the calories for the health-program people, right?"

"Not only for them, but for the modeling students as well. The formula is different since the students only aim at maintaining their weight, but we want them to eat nutritious, healthy foods. Few young people can maintain a slim and trim body without paying attention to what they eat, and I will not tolerate anorexic or bulimic behavior."

She went on, "Then we have the cook, Isandro Jimenez, with his kitchen crew and Dolores Garcia, the head housekeeper who's in charge of the domestic help. Both these jobs are also obvious."

Andi thought about all this information and then asked, "Does the principal, I think you said Emma Demitris, know why I'm here?"

"No. At first I planned to tell her, but then decided against it. Don't get me wrong, I trust Emma 100% and she is discreet, but I think she might involuntarily treat you differently from the rest of the students if she knew."

"But Mr. Camden knows?"

"Certainly. My husband and I are a team. Is there other information you need?"

"I'll get to know the students, and I'll find a way to mingle with the clients, but getting to meet the patrons won't be easy, I reckon. Can you tell me a little about each, and why they're here?"

"Under normal circumstances I would tell you, absolutely not! The patrons' privacy is our top priority. We emphasize to students and clients that they are not to bother the patrons. Paparazzi have tried to gain access to some of the high-profile celebrities, and I assure you, they get no farther than my office. In order for you to do your job properly, I will make an exception. The quicker you solve our mystery, the better for everyone concerned, including the patrons.

"At the moment there are three patrons here: Brant Ronnquist, Adam Applebee and Valencia Kirkland. We expect a fourth, Chad Richmond, to arrive in the next few days. Dr. Ronnquist is a surgeon. He was overworked, stressed out and close to a nervous breakdown when he came to us about a month ago. He is here to relax and enjoy his hobby of bird-watching. Mr. Applebee is a writer. The reason for his stay is to write his manuscript without being distracted by the outside world. We hardly see him; he mostly stays in his room and wants to be left alone. I'm sure you know that Ms. Kirkland is an actress. She wanted to get away from the public. Ms. Kirkland and Mr. Applebee are regulars, by the way. The actress comes once or twice a year, and the writer, whenever he can't concentrate at home. Mr. Richmond is the CEO of a major corporation. You don't need to know any particulars about him. He wasn't here during our problems and therefore cannot be involved."

Andi said, "Mrs. Huber checked out your place on the Web. There is plenty of information about the modeling school and the health program, but no mention of the patrons. We're curious; how do you find them?"

Mrs. Camden replied, "We don't advertise having a facility for patrons. That side of Optimum House is strictly passed on by word of mouth. Part of the big draw for our patrons is that we keep their stay here confidential, so we don't want the general public to know about such a program."

The door opened, and a man in his forties stood in the doorway. He apologized, "Oh, sorry. I'll come back later."

Iris said, "We're almost through. Give me a few more minutes."

The man nodded, and as the door closed behind him, Iris remarked, "That was Ralph Smith, the instructor for the male modeling students." And she asked, "We *are* almost through?"

Andi said, "Sure thing, Mrs. Camden." And after a slight pause, "So you have male students enrolled, and they have a different teacher?"

"Yes. At the moment there are only two. We are starting the practical instructions today. When it comes to practicum, the male students' needs are different from the females'."

"How is that?"

"Our sessions start with theory, and that part of the curriculum takes about a month. The theoretical classes can be easily applied to both male and female students. So until last Friday, during the theory, all students participated together in Emma's classroom. Today, the practicum starts and the male instructor teaches the two male students. They have much shorter sessions anyway, since makeup application and so forth is omitted in their course."

"Gotcha." Then Andi asked, "How long does the modeling school last? I mean - -"

"I know what you mean," Iris interrupted. "We have two sessions a year at three months each: the first from beginning of April to beginning of July and the other from beginning of September to beginning of December. The time in between gives me a chance to set up appointments with top agencies for students with great potential, and I might take one or two to modeling conventions."

"Do you keep the same time schedule for the health program?"

"That is being operated around the clock, except when we close the entire facility from mid-December until mid-March. Clients stay as long as they want, or until they have the results they strive for."

"And patrons come and go as they please?"

"Precisely."

Iris looked at her watch, and Andi felt sure her time was up. So she quickly said, "Just one more thing, Mrs. Camden. Does the academic teacher, I forgot her name, give private tutoring?"

"Yes, Mrs. Brackenbury gives private tutoring lessons on the side. Why do you ask?"

"I'd like to get some tutoring."

Surprised, Iris inquired, "Haven't you finished high school?"

"Sure did, but how else can I tackle the lady?"

"That can be arranged, of course." She checked her watch again and said, "They're having mid-day break at the school, so Mrs. Demitris will show you around and take you to your room."

Chapter 9

Emma Demitris guided the new student on a quick tour around the first floor of the main building. The principal was tall and fit, with light-brown straight hair in a bobbed style. The former model was also in her late thirties, like Iris Camden. However, Emma did not possess the magnetism that was characteristic of her employer. As she escorted Andi out of the administrative office, she gave her a scrutinizing look but didn't say a thing. They walked along the corridor past the kitchen on their left, and the library to the right.

Mrs. Demitris said, "You missed the entire introduction and theory program. I'm surprised Mrs. Camden is letting you start this late into the course."

"I'm a fast learner."

"We'll see about that." Then she pointed out, "Here is the dining hall," and as she pushed the portal open, Andi got a glimpse of people sitting around large rectangular tables having their lunch before the principal pulled it close again. Then they moved on to the opposite side of the hallway, where Andi got a peek at the gym, sauna, and pool. An aqua-fit lesson was coming to an end in the pool area. Other than that, not much was happening since most people were taking their lunch break. The conference, recreation, and class rooms were equally deserted. The door to one of the small offices at the end of the corridor stood open where the dietitian sat laboring over her calculation charts.

Demitris stuck her head in and said, "Nadine, I know you're busy on Mondays with client evaluations, but can you make time for this new student in the afternoon?"

Nadine Dugat replied, "No problem, I can squeeze her in."

As they climbed the stairs to the upper floor, Emma said, "All the single bedrooms are taken, so you'll have to share your quarters with a roommate."

"Fine by me," Andi replied. She silently welcomed the fact, hoping the young woman she'd be rooming with could help her with getting a feel for the place.

They walked down the hallway past several doors on either side, painted in different colors. Emma came to a halt in front of a pink one, opened it, and motioned Andi in. The room was furnished with two double beds and a nightstand next to each, a chest of drawers, an entertainment center with TV and DVD player and two small desks.

Andi remarked, "This is much nicer than I expected." Then she walked to the window and, looking out, exclaimed, "And with a view to the lake!"

Emma smiled and said, "Glad you like it. Looks like the bed nearer the window is taken by your roommate, Cyrilla Washington, so this one is yours," and she pointed to the one closer to the door. "I told Cyrilla to make room for your things. Let me check to be sure there are fresh towels for you."

Andi followed her into the bathroom. There was a double sink, a tub and a separate shower. A large bath towel, washcloth and shower cap hung from the towel bar. Pantyhose, a lacy bra and a pair of matching panties were drying on a small folding rack.

The principal motioned to a shelf with neatly folded towels and washcloths, saying, "Plenty of clean ones for you."

As they walked back to the bedroom she asked, "Have you had lunch?"

Andi shook her head.

"It's served from noon to 2:00 in the dining hall. I'll let you get settled now, and then go have lunch. Later in the afternoon, you can see Ms. Dugat in her office. She'll weigh, measure and assess you. There's no sense in coming to class today. The afternoon session will already be in progress by the time the dietitian is through with you. You'll start your training tomorrow. Be in the runway classroom wearing high heels at 10:00 a.m. sharp."

"Sure thing, Mrs. Demitris."

Descending the stairs, Emma chuckled inwardly. When Iris told her about a new student from Louisiana named Antoinette LeJeune, she had formed a vague picture of a Southern Belle, all proper and genteel. Therefore, she had been shocked when she first saw Andi, but then she had gotten beyond the getup and had looked at her more closely and suddenly felt that the young woman had potential. She was entirely different from any of the numerous aspiring models she had come across, and therein lay her charm. She needed lots of work, but it could be done. All this went through her mind in seconds. By the time she reached the bottom step, she had decided that, yes, Andi was definitely worth the effort.

Chapter 10

Minutes later Andi was on her way to lunch. As she walked along the upstairs corridor, she looked at each door with amusement. Every color imaginable was represented, from basic red, blue, green, orange and yellow to shades of pink, lavender, chartreuse, mauve, turquoise and olive. She mused that painting the bedroom doors different colors was a smart idea; how else would she ever find her room again?

She opened the giant portal to the dining hall and stood at the entrance. She had only glanced at the large room when Mrs. Demitris showed her around, and now took the time to observe it more thoroughly. There were four large, rectangular tables forming two rows parallel to the length of the room, seating about ten people each. There was a smaller rectangular table placed a fair distance away from the others and a round table at the end corner of the room. A luncheon buffet was placed in front of each of the occupied tables. The window panels, stretching along the entire outside wall, and the Renoir prints hanging on the opposite wall gave the place more of a hotel conference room feeling, rather than an institutional mess hall effect. The spring flower bouquets placed on each table added to the room's atmosphere.

At present, students were seated at two of the large tables and clients at another. The time was just after one o'clock, and some of the chairs had already been vacated. At the smaller table Valencia Kirkland sat between Jeffrey and Iris Camden. The animated Ms. Kirkland chatted happily away, turning her head from one to the other of her hosts, gesticulating with her ring-adorned hands. The staff - - consisting of Emma Demitris, Kathleen Brakenbury, and Nadine Dugat - - lunched at the round table.

Andi walked over to where the students sat and then stood still, not sure where to go.

A bubbly blonde jumped out of her chair, grabbed Andi by the hand and said, "Here. Take the seat next to mine. Mrs. Demitris told us we were getting a new student. You must be her. I'm Susie, by the way. Go fix yourself a plate, there's plenty left."

"Thanks, Susie. My name's Andi."

Andi felt suddenly starved and loaded her plate with mixed salads, tuna and a piece of whole wheat bread. She filled a glass with water from the pitcher provided and carried both to her place setting. Then she dug in heartily.

The student sitting on the other side of Susie leaned across her friend's head and shouted, "I'm Olivia. Pleased to meet you, Andi, and how's your love life?"

Andi had taken a big bite of tuna and had her mouth full. She almost choked.

Susie gave Olivia a playful nudge and said, "Cut it out, will you!" And turning to Andi she stated, "Never mind Olivia. She's nuts."

Olivia prompted, "Nuts, did you say?" And wiggling a bit in her chair she continued, "Where? I thought all the boys were gone!"

Susie, following her own advice, ignored Olivia's remark and asked Andi, "Are you coming to class this afternoon?"

"I start tomorrow."

"I'll see you then." And she turned to her friend, saying, "Come on, Olivia, let's go."

When Andi had finished her lunch, she looked around the room. Mrs. Brackenbury was left alone at the round table. The small table where the Camdens had sat with the actress was empty, and most of the students and clients had either gone or were getting ready to leave. At Andi's table there was only one other person still seated, way at the other end. Andi looked over at her. The young woman's head was bent over a pad of sketch paper, her face partially hidden by a strand of dark hair. Then she looked up and seemed to concentrate on Andi. The dark eyes momentarily half closed, making them appear slanted. Then she bent back down to the work in front of her.

Andi was about to clear away her dishes and get up when the dark-haired student strolled over to her. She handed her the sketch, and said, "I'm Nancy Zagarian."

Andi looked down at the artwork and was flabbergasted. She gawked at an extremely good pencil drawing of herself.

"This is mighty good; you're quite an artist."

"You may keep it."

"Thank you so much!"

Andi studied the sketch once more, and when she looked up again, Nancy had quietly disappeared.

Chapter 11

Ambling in the direction of the dietitian's office Andi thought, weigh, measure and assess. Sounds like buying a racehorse! Do I open my mouth for a teeth check?

The door to Nadine Dugat's office was closed. Andi was about to knock, when it was flung open and a client came out, a happy grin on his face.

"I lost 4 ¼ pounds this week!"

Andi gave him a high-five and then went inside.

Nadine Dugat sat at her desk, engrossed in paperwork. She looked up when Andi entered and said, "You're the new student? Take a seat."

"Yes, ma'am."

"Please don't call me that! Do I look like a ma'am?"

Andi studied the dietitian thoroughly. The woman was in her twenties. Her face was not pretty, but interesting. A long narrow nose hovered over a mouth that was a bit too wide. The deep-set eyes, peering at her through gold-rimmed glasses, were gray as steel. She had tied her blondish-brown hair into a ponytail.

Seeing no wedding ring on the lady's finger Andi asked, "What do I call you?"

"Ms. Dugat will work." And she continued, "Let me check if you're already entered into our system. Your last name is?"

"LeJeune."

Nadine got busy on her keyboard and then said, "LeJeune, Antoinette," and set the printer into motion. Then she handed the printout to Andi.

"Please verify that the information is correct."

Andi glanced at it. She was looking at a form with the top part already filled in with her name, address and phone number, gender, date and place of birth, race, eye and hair color. Then there was a title, Physical Assessment, followed by fields not yet filled in.

She handed the form back, saying, "Looks okay to me."

"What size slacks do you wear, Antoinette?"

"Four, and please call me Andi."

"As you wish. What dress size?"

"Whatever fits."

The dietitian glared at her and said, "What kind of an answer is that?"

"I'm not trying to be disrespectful, Ms. Dugat, but I don't look at the size. When I see a dress that I wanna buy, I try it on. If it fits I'll get it."

Nadine scrutinized her with an expert's eye and then wrote down "size 4."

"How tall are you?"

"5'9", I think."

"How much do you weigh?"

When she did not get an answer, she looked up from the form and said, "It's not a tough question, Andi. What do you weigh on your scale?"

"I don't have one."

Totally taken aback, Nadine said, "You're kidding!"

Andi shrugged and remarked, "I thought *you*'re going to do the measuring and weighing."

"True, but we like to know what the students think they measure and weigh. Our scale is 100% accurate, and we certainly keep the records according to it."

Nadine wrote a question mark into the field "Student Scale" and said, "Please take your clothes off and step onto the scale over there," and she pointed to the large medical scale standing next to one wall.

When Andi stood on it in her bra and panties, Nadine stationed herself in front and lowered the bar down to the crown of Andi's head, reading the numbers aloud.

"You are 5'8 ¾" tall." Then she flipped the weights around on the scale to make them balance and announced, "And you weigh exactly 118 pounds."

Andi was not sure if she was expected to be upset or pleased with the result, so to be on the safe side she refrained from commenting.

Nadine said, "Now to your body composition," and she went over to a cabinet and took an instrument out of the drawer. The tool looked odd and with a little imagination could be called gun-shaped. It had a handgrip on one end, a half-moon scale at the other with pivoted tips extending from it like fangs.

When she approached with the instrument in hand, Andi asked, "What are you planning on doing to me with this thing?"

"It's called a skinfold caliper and it measures subcutaneous tissue."

"Come again?"

"That's body fat."

"Gotcha! So you're going to pinch me with that?"

"Correct."

"Where?"

"Your triceps and hip area."

Before Nadine started the procedure, she looked Andi over and stated, "You have more upper arm and thigh muscle than most modeling students. Do you work out?"

Andi thought about chasing Duchess down Wilshire Boulevard and replied, "Some." And she added, "Is that good or bad?"

Nadine smiled for the first time since Andi had stepped into her office. Then she confided, "Personally, I like an athletic look. Most people in charge of modeling agencies, however, don't seem to share my opinion."

Andi thought that she'd better get used to hearing what model agencies liked or disliked.

Then the dietitian said, "Hold up your right arm, please."

As Andi did so, Nadine applied the skinfold caliper to the back part of the upper arm and squeezed until she got a reading. Then she did the same to the hip. Lastly she pulled a measuring tape out of her pocket and proceeded to wrap it around Andi's thigh.

She wrote the result figures down, "subcutaneous tissue; triceps: 27 millimeters; hip: 8 millimeters; thigh measurement: 46 centimeters," and murmured, "Excellent numbers."

While Andi was putting her clothes back on, Nadine studied the form and then said, "You're in good shape and should be pleased with your data." And she continued, "What kind of a diet do you follow?"

"Diet?"

"What do you generally eat?"

Andi's first impulse was to reply, whatever is on sale. Then she remembered Mrs. Huber's instructions, *Live the role.* So she said meekly, "I'm ashamed to say that I don't follow any special diet."

Nadine looked at the printout once more and stated, "You are 18, and so far you've been lucky. Eating whatever you feel like will not do in the long run. I'm not only referring to your modeling career aspirations but also to your health and well-being."

"I understand, Ms. Dugat."

"Any allergies?"

"None that I know of."

Nadine Dugat's last statement was, "I'm prescribing a maintenance diet for you."

Chapter 12

Andi stood in her room and looked out the window. On this mild and sunny day, the water was calm and a deep blue-green. A fishing boat anchored a short distance away was swaying gently in the soft breeze. She judged the lake's width to be about half a mile, and she could make out a cluster of buildings along the opposite shore. That must be the village of Big Bear Lake, she concluded.

She turned away from the window, walked over to her bed and stretched out on the comforter. Then she closed her eyes. Images of her day, so far, came to mind like flashbacks in a movie. Her ride over to the Big Bear area, getting "enrolled" by Mrs. Camden, Mrs. Demitris showing her around the place, the lunch scene - -

Andi's daydream was interrupted when the door opened and in glided a young woman. There was poise and grace in the stride of her long legs. She was about six feet tall, had a gorgeous face with high cheekbones, carried herself like royalty and was African American.

She exclaimed, "'Who's been sleeping in my bed?' said Goldilocks."

Andi stared. Then she burst out laughing.

"Hi! I'm Cyrilla Washington, your roommate. And there goes my privacy!"

"Hello there, Cyrilla. Andi's my name. Sorry to invade your space!"

"Just kidding. I don't mind the company. You don't snore, do you?"

"Hope not."

"You from Louisiana?"

Andi nodded. "And you?"

"Sweet Georgia," Cyrilla replied.

"Us Southerners best stick together, then."

"You're all settled in?"

"I haven't unpacked. I waited for you to show me my territory."

"So where's your luggage?"

Andi pointed to the touring bag next to her bed.

Cyrilla laughed and said, "A compact woman!" Then she noticed the helmets and cried out, "Mercy! That big, ugly motorcycle in the parking lot is yours?"

"Sure is, and it's a beauty!"

Cyrilla shrugged and remarked, "When I had the room to myself, my things were scattered all over, but Mrs. Demitris told me to make room for you, so I cleared out your desk. It's the one over there, without the laptop. I also emptied the top drawer of the dresser."

Then she walked over to the wardrobe closet and opened it. The entire space was taken up with her clothing. She shoved some of the hangers to one side, leaving a cavity of roughly a foot and asked, "Enough room for you?"

"That'll do."

Andi got off the bed and, starting to put away her belongings, asked, "You don't have any classes this afternoon?"

"Had a doctor's appointment in San Bernardino to get my allergy shots. I just got back." And looking at her watch she stated, "It's close to three o'clock. I'm taking the rest of the day off. Today's lesson is all about posture, so I don't think I'll miss much."

Andi said, "I missed the whole introduction and theory. Was there anything important?"

"Mostly what agencies are looking for," she grinned, "or *not* looking for." Then she said, "You'll be fine. The practical part is starting now."

Andi had put her tops, underwear and pantyhose in the chest of drawers and her small objects in the desk. Now she placed two pairs of black shoes - - one flats, the other pumps - - at the bottom of the closet and hung three pairs of trousers, a couple of skirts and a dress on the vacant hangers.

Glancing at the long row of shoes and exquisite outfits that filled the rest of the closet, all arranged neatly according to color, Andi said, "You must have rich parents. I mean, this school doesn't come cheap."

"Do I look like I was brought up with a silver spoon?" she replied sarcastically. Then she went on, "My folks were poor."

"Dead?"

"Might as well be. I never knew who my father was. My momma met a Jamaican when I was 12 and took off with him to Jamaica."

"I'm sorry."

Cyrilla replied, "Don't be. I never saw eye to eye with Momma."

"Who brought you up, then?"

"Granny. I do love Granny. To answer your question, I got plenty of money from a lawsuit settlement." And clearly not wanting to disclose the particulars of the suit, she said, "And where did you get the cash for the tuition?"

Of course, Andi could not tell her that she was a hired hand and didn't pay for the schooling or room-and-board, but answered truthfully, "My daddy left me an inheritance." Then she shared a little about her background.

There was one last item in the touring bag, but Andi did not take it out. She made a bet with herself that her roommate was not the nosy type.

Cyrilla had watched her unpack and said, "Can't believe all that stuff came out of your small bag!"

"Just like magic!" Andi snickered.

She placed her seemingly empty touring bag next to the shoes and piled the two helmets on top. She was just about to close the wardrobe when she suddenly burst out, "Shit! My goggles! Where are they?"

Cyrilla said, "Don't let Mrs. Demitris hear you use that kind of language."

Andi paid no attention and repeated, "My goggles are gone," and stormed out of the room.

Chapter 13

Peter Huber glanced at his spouse across the table for two. They were having dinner at *Chez Tante Jeanne*, their favorite restaurant. Maurice had suggested they try the venison, and it had been an excellent choice.

Now, lingering over coffee, Peter said, "I can tell you're worried, Regula. Is your mind up in Big Bear?"

She nodded. "I guess it shows."

"Are you getting cold feet about sending the young woman up?"

She sighed, "I think Andi can handle the job. In lots of ways she's mature for someone her age. I believe that losing her father so early in life has made her strong and independent. Traveling alone across country on a motorcycle certainly takes guts! Although unsophisticated, I think she's bright and to a certain extent street smart."

"So what's bothering you?"

"She hasn't called yet."

"Was she supposed to?"

"I told her she needed to report to me and not to act on her own. I left it up to her when to call."

Peter asked, "So what's the problem?"

"It is Tuesday evening. She's been there for two entire days. I had expected a call by now."

"You were never a mother hen with our kids, so why start now with this young woman?"

"You're right. I just hope I didn't throw her to the wolves."

"Give it a rest, Regula. She'll be fine."

His wife smiled and said, "Okay, let's change the subject. How's your novel coming along?"

"It's not coming along at all. I'm stuck. I've rewritten the same chapter umpteen times; the more I revise, the worse it gets. I'm starting to think the whole story is idiotic."

"That bad? Maybe it needs a woman's touch. If I knew the outline of the plot, I could help."

Peter chuckled, "You never give up, do you?"

"Never!"

Chapter 14

The call came Wednesday evening.

R. A. Huber declared, "Andi! It's about time!"

"Had to get a feel for the place before I could tell you about it."

"So what can you report so far?"

"When you told me about the weird set-up here, the place sounded like a circus. Now I see that the show is well organized."

Huber said, "How so?"

"You already know about the different groups, so I'll just tell you how it works. There are 18 modeling school students, not including me, two of them male. Out of the 16 females, 12 are still in high school. The two male students have a different curriculum and their own teacher. They are both high-school graduates and hold part-time jobs on the side. The girls are together in the modeling training, but the four older students don't have to attend the academic classes.

"Here's how it's done: The 12 kids start their day at 7:45 in the morning with scholastic classes. They get a 15-minute break before the modeling session starts at 10:00, when the older four students join them. From noon until 2:00 in the afternoon all get their lunch break. Then from 2:00 to 4:00 the modeling class continues. At 4:00, the older students are done for the day and the kids go back to academic classes after a break. Their day is finally done at 5:30."

"I see."

Andi continued, "I'm not sure how the day is divided for the health-program clients. I know they have all sorts

of fitness programs, like working out in the gym, aqua-
fit lessons and going on nature hikes. Patrons can do
whatever they want. Mealtimes are the same for all three
groups. The continental breakfast is from 7:00 to 9:30,
a buffet lunch is served from noon to 2:00 and a formal
dinner is at 6:30. Patrons can have their meals delivered to
the room if they don't wanna come to the dining hall."

Huber said, "I agree. The place seems well organized.
How is it done with the food? I can imagine the students
and the patrons don't eat the same meals as do the weight
watchers."

"The groups sit at different tables. People trying to lose
weight have a special diet, the students get a maintenance
one, and the patrons can choose either of the two, or order
whatever they like." And she added, "I'm surprised; the
chow really tastes good!"

Then she said, "Now, boss, you wanna know about the
folks I've met and talked to so far?"

"Right, and tell me what you think of each person."

"You've met Mrs. Camden, so I won't describe her. She
cooperates with me, because after all, she wants to find the
bad guy in a hurry. She sure is catering to the patrons. No
one is to bother them! By the way, she doesn't advertise
the patron part of the show. That's why you couldn't find
anything about them on the Web. You also know Mr.
Camden. He's a sweetheart. I feel sorry for him; he's got
no one to talk shop with except for me."

"You interviewed him?"

"Not exactly. I went to the gym to work out." She
chuckled and added, "Have to be careful not to overdo it;
modeling agencies don't like muscles, I'm told!"

"What did you mean by talking shop?"

"Football."

"Of course!"

Then she said, "I'm sure you've noticed that he's limping. I think he's in pain when he walks, so I asked him about it. Seems he banged up his leg pretty good and had a knee replacement, but there wasn't much the doctors could do about his kneecap at the time. The old injury will bother him for the rest of his life, I reckon."

She continued, "Mrs. Demitris is a mighty fine instructor as far as I can tell. She gives all students a good run for their money, not just the promising ones. If I was seriously considering a modeling career, I'd trust her judgment. Ms. Dugat, the dietitian, is all business. I think she knows her stuff, though. I'll meet the academic teacher, Mrs. Brackenbury, tomorrow."

"How do you know you'll meet her tomorrow?"

"I'm getting tutoring."

Huber couldn't suppress an audible laugh, and then said, "You don't lack ingenuity!"

Andi went on with her report; "I made friends with my roommate, Cyrilla Washington. I like her; she's easy to talk to and she can also show me the ropes. Cyrilla's a natural. I'm sure she'll be a supermodel. I also met the other three older students. Susie Seales is a cute, bubbly blonde who loves the school and all it stands for. She's the first to admit that at 5'6", 127 pounds, and a good-size chest, chances of a modeling career are slim for her. She's having fun, though, and everybody likes her. Her friend, on the other hand, Olivia Volmer, gets on people's nerves. She's a nymphomaniac and never shuts up about it. Susie told me that the only reason she is good friends with Olivia and tolerates her strange behavior is because she knows about her strict upbringing. Apparently her parents have jobs that require them to travel the world, and so they stuck Olivia in a boarding school where she was brought up by nuns. Then there's Nancy Zagarian.

Nancy is shy and dreams of becoming an artist, but her mother is the pushy kind and has different plans for her.

"The rest of the students are harder for me to get to know. I see the girls during class, but they don't have much free time. They're busy with academic schooling, homework and all. I haven't seen either of the male students. So far, I've met one person in the health-program. Her name is Paula Parsall. She has a great sense of humor and is a chatterbox. I've gotten lots of chit-chat out of her already."

"Like what?"

"Oh, mostly gossip. According to her, one of the guys has a drinking problem, two are carrying on an affair, and another is smuggling in junk food. She told me that she caught several students smoking, all minors. She also seemed to know secrets about some of the patrons. She said she'd heard from a reliable source that the surgeon had recently botched an operation. She also took Valencia Kirkland apart by telling me in detail about some scandal the actress was involved in while married to her third husband. I'm sure she got that out of the tabloids. She claimed that Jeffrey Camden supplied all the money for starting the modeling school and that Mrs. Camden was having an affair. All pure gossip, I'm sure."

She concluded, "That's all the people I've tackled, so far."

"You've learned a lot, considering you've only been there since Monday. Were there any new thefts, or has anyone mentioned them and the other incidents?"

"Uh-huh. My goggles got swiped soon as I got here!"

"Really! Did they turn up again?"

"Nope."

"Tell me the goggles story."

Andi said, "I'm sure I had them when I first walked into Mrs. Camden's office because I remember putting them at the edge of her desk. After that, I don't know what happened to them. I've racked my brain trying to remember if I had them with me when leaving the administrative office, but it's no use. So I'm pretty sure I left them on the desk. Anyhow, some two hours later, I missed them when unpacking my bag. So I rushed down to Mrs. Camden's office. The goggles weren't there anymore, but she said that she saw them on her desk while talking with me.

"Mrs. Camden left her office at the same time I did when Mrs. Demitris came to fetch me for a tour of the place. I saw her leave, telling the instructor who was waiting for her in the hall that she was on her way to lunch and she'd meet him in her office an hour later. She didn't remember seeing the goggles on her desk after lunch when she and the instructor entered the office together."

"So what does that tell you, Andi?"

"That the thief could only have pinched my goggles during one hour's time. I went on the tour at about 12:45 p.m., and Mrs. Camden said that she got back to her office at 1:45 p.m." And she added, "I made a big stink too, said they were polarized and expensive, making sure everybody heard about the theft."

"Did you get the reaction you hoped for?"

"You guessed it, boss! People, mostly students, talked to me about some of the other things stolen."

"Did you get any useful information?"

"Not much, actually."

"Which of the students mentioned the previous occurrences?"

"Cyrilla, mostly. She said that there was evil doings going on in the place. She was still shocked that somebody cut her favorite dress into shreds. She also commented on some of the other thefts, but didn't tell me anything more than I already learned from you. Susie mentioned the diamond necklace, and Olivia told me the alarm clock story, getting off her sex kick for once."

"What are the students' reactions to the happenings at Optimum House?"

Andi replied, "I think in the beginning they thought it was funny. Especially the disappearance of Mrs. Demitris's alarm clock seemed to have tickled them. Olivia said that the student body knew the modeling teacher was a heavy sleeper, and they all found it hilarious that someone was able to sneak into her bedroom while she was asleep and snatch the clock. Now I think they're all starting to get scared."

There was a pause on the line, and then Mrs. Huber asked, "Have you formed any theories as to your goggles?"

"No. At first I thought it'd be easy to eliminate some people. My goggles were snatched in the short time of an hour. I couldn't cross anyone off my list, though. They were stolen during the lunch break, so anyone could've walked into Mrs. Camden's office and taken them. She didn't lock it up. Nobody ever locks any doors in the entire place, I've noticed. I wasn't in the dining hall the whole hour, so checking who was there at the same time is no help."

Then she stated, "That's all I have to report."

Huber said, "You've accumulated lots of information in a short amount of time. I'm proud of you, Andi."

"Thanks! My classes are only from ten to noon and from two to four, so I've got lots of free time. Might as well earn my keep as your assistant!"

"And you've given this case a lot of thought, already. Keep thinking!"

"Yes, ma'am!"

"Until your next report, then." They were about to hang up when Huber inquired, "How are you faring with your modeling lessons?"

"Today, Mrs. Demitris used me as an example of how *not* to walk on the runway!"

Chapter 15

Regula took a moment to think over the rap session that had just ended before she joined her husband in the living room.

Peter teased, "I read the entire L.A. Times while you were on the phone."

She smiled and replied, "Our long talk was not in vain!" And she continued, "Andi is doing a good job. I'm impressed."

"Was it only yesterday that you were ready to send out the troops after her?"

"I was wrong."

"Have there been more incidents since she got there?"

"Affirmative! Andi is the newest theft victim. Her goggles were taken shortly after she arrived."

"The perpetrator sure isn't wasting time! What else did she say?"

"All right, Peter. You're dying to hear Andi's entire report. So here goes," and Regula related a condensed version of the phone conversation.

Then her spouse remarked, "Don't you think it's about time they start locking their doors?"

"Good point, but that might not be practical. I'm sure the domestics need to have access to each room. The place is not a hotel where the cleaning crew has a pass key."

"I hadn't thought of that." Then he said, "Iris Camden seems to pamper the patrons excessively. I was already aware of that when you told the Camden story after their visit to your office, and now Andi seems to stress it also."

"It is a necessity. I'm positive the patrons pay a good portion of the bills."

"Oh?"

"To run and maintain such a place takes an enormous amount of money. Besides providing room and board, paying the staff and domestics' salaries, and maintenance of the building, there are all sorts of extra costs. Remember, Mrs. Camden brings in photographers, masseurs, manicurists, and so forth. She needs those patrons in order to show a profit. I imagine that the modeling school and weight-control program isn't cheap, but there has to be a limit to what can be charged to students and clients. So you see, making the patrons happy and coming back for more is a top priority to keep Optimum House running."

"Yes, that makes sense." Then he said, "That Parsall woman sounds like she sticks her nose into everyone else's business. Some of the things she supposedly ferreted out are harmless enough, like catching the girls smoking, for instance, but what she said about the doctor is a serious accusation."

"I agree. Gossiping seems to be the woman's hobby. So we have to treat her chatter as gossip, not the gospel truth. "

Peter said, "Speaking of smoking, is it getting any easier?"

"A little."

"Are you wearing the patch?"

"Of course."

"How much longer until you won't need it anymore?"

"The way it's going, I'll wear it for the rest of my life."

He said, "I suffer too, you know."

"Really?"

"Sure. I have to put up with your withdrawal moods!"

Regula changed the subject and asked, "Are you still having problems with your manuscript?"

"Major problems. I don't want to talk about it."

After a pause, she wanted to know, "Are we doing something tonight?"

"What do you have in mind?"

"Chess, Go, Backgammon or Trivial Pursuit. Your call, Peter."

He gave her *the look* and said, "I have a better idea!"

"There's always that," Regula agreed, and as she led him down the hall toward their bedroom, she murmured, "So it's the writer and not the story that needs a woman's touch."

Chapter 16

Thursday morning at dawn Adam Applebee woke up from another night's restless sleep. How many hours had he actually slept? Three, four at best? The characters in his current manuscript had popped in and out of his mind like demons, urging him to change the lousy plot. They hadn't left him alone, begrudging him a decent night's rest.

Adam lingered in bed and stared up at the ceiling. Why wasn't he able to concentrate and be productive like he had been on previous visits to this place? The perfect peace and tranquility here had always inspired his creativity in the past. So why wasn't it working now? He knew the reason, at least the most crucial one. It was Helen. Why hadn't he seen it coming? And if he had, would he have done anything to prevent it? Probably not; his entire lifestyle would have had to change.

He sighed and continued musing. If he was honest with himself, he had to admit that it wasn't so much the fact that Helen had left but what she said as she was leaving. The image came back to him again and again. She had opened the door to his study, suitcase in hand, "I'm leaving you, Adam." He had been totally taken aback and like an idiot asked, "Right now?" She had replied, "Yes, I'm picking up the kids from school and then we're off." He had been speechless for a second and then managed to ask, "Another man?" She had shaken her head and stated, "I doubt you'll miss us much, or even realize that we're gone. Your books are your family, Adam. I never could understand how a cold fish like you could write such wonderful stories, full of sensitive characters. The tender love scene in your last book brought tears of jealousy to my eyes."

The last words she threw at him, right after the part about her lawyer would be in touch, was, "You won't have to go to Optimum House any longer to concentrate. No one will bother you here. You can have this house all to yourself; we're not coming back."

Well, he had come to Optimum House anyway, and now he couldn't concentrate here. What irony! He thought back to last night's dinner. That too had been less than satisfactory. He had hoped to have Iris to himself, but that irritating actress demanded most of her attention. The trip down to the dining hall certainly hadn't been worth the trouble. Might as well eat dinner in my room too, not just breakfast and lunch, he thought, sadly.

Adam finally pulled himself out of bed and headed for the bathroom. When he had finished showering and was toweling himself off, he heard a knock at the door.

"Just leave my breakfast on the table, please," he hollered.

The maid came into his suite and placed the tray on the table. She poured a glass of juice but left the coffee in the pot and the domed metal lid over the food in order to keep it hot. Then she left.

A couple of minutes later, Adam walked into the spacious room. The evening before, he had left his order of bacon, scrambled eggs, toast, orange juice and coffee in the little box outside his door. When he saw the breakfast tray on the table, he suddenly felt hungry and sat down. He took a sip of orange juice and poured coffee into his cup, then grabbed the lid to uncover the food - -

He jerked backward in shock and yelled, "What the hell?"

A pair of ugly goggles sat on his bacon and eggs.

Chapter 17

Between the Camdens' suite and the gym there was a beauty salon. Andi sat at the manicurist's table facing the young Asian woman who had just applied a French manicure to her fingertips. At the opposite side of the room, a student was getting a cut and style. Andi was about to immerse her feet into warm, bubbling water for her pedicure when Valencia Kirkland made an entrance.

The actress drifted into the room and addressed the manicurist, "My nails are a mess. Do you have time for a fill, Mollie?"

"Right away, Ms. Kirkland." And to Andi, "I hope you don't mind waiting with the pedicure."

"No problem," Andi replied and moved over to the 'waiting seat.'

Valencia smiled and slid into the vacated chair. The blonde celebrity was forty-two but looked ten years younger. Although slender, she sported a generous bosom and a shapely derriere. Like most people in her line of work, she was performing even when not on the job. The world was her stage.

She flipped her long hair back with a swift motion of the hand and focused her wide-set baby-blue eyes on the manicurist, saying, "I can't make up my mind today; you choose the color for me."

"Sure, Ms. Kirkland. Fuchsia goes well with the outfit you have on."

"You think so?"

"Or possibly a softer pink."

This kind of banter went back and forth between the two. Andi had a clear view of the actress from where she sat. She watched her animated facial expressions but didn't pay attention to the conversation. She was trying to figure out a way to talk with the lady. Not an easy task, since patrons were to be left in peace.

Suddenly, Valencia Kirkland made eye contact with Andi and said, "You're new here. Are you a student?"

"Yes, ma'am. Got here Monday."

"Oh, a Southerner!" Instantly, the actress switched to a Southern drawl and remarked, "I love your hair; it has such a lustrous sheen. What's the color?"

"I reckon you'd call it auburn."

Valencia laughed, "What I meant is, where do you get it done or what's the code if you color it yourself?"

Andi replied, "It's natural."

"Lucky for you! Most women would kill to have hair like that."

"Thank you!" And she added, "I'm glad you got your necklace back."

"So you've heard about that. News surely travels fast. You came on Monday, you said. Are you the young woman whose sunglasses were stolen?"

"Goggles, not sunglasses."

"Whatever. Have they been recovered?"

"No, ma'am."

"You'll get them back eventually. There's a person among us with a warped sense of humor."

Then the actress lost interest in Andi and returned her attention to the matter at hand, her acrylic nails.

Soon it was Andi's turn to get a pedicure. She didn't know what to expect, but the procedure was not unpleasant. When Mollie rubbed the bottom of her feet with a pumice stone, Andi giggled and tried not to pull away.

Mollie asked, "Ticklish?"

"And how!"

"Is this your first pedicure?"

"Uh-huh."

When the manicurist had finished, Andi looked down at her bright-red toenails and thought to herself, I'm getting to be a real girly girl!

Then Mollie said, "Now to your eyebrow waxing."

"Waxing?"

The woman beckoned, "This way, please," and Andi had no choice but to follow her to a curtained cubicle at the end of the room. Mollie drew open the curtain and motioned for Andi to lie down on the narrow bed, pulling the drapery shut behind them. The space in the cubicle was sparse. There was just enough room for the bed-like furniture in the center and leeway around it for a person to move about.

As Andi stretched out on the cot, Mollie turned on a lamp above her head, adjusting it so that the strong light shone directly into Andi's eyes.

Mollie said, "Close your eyes and relax."

"Sure thing," Andi replied.

She felt a warm liquid being applied above and below her eyebrows, followed by a strip of tape. Yeah, she thought, this is relaxing. Then, without the slightest warning, the tape above one eyebrow was pulled off.

"Shit!" she cried out. The pain was excruciating for a second.

"Hold still, please! I've got to do the rest."

There followed three more pulls, one above the other brow and one below each. Despite knowing now what to expect, Andi's body still twitched with every yanking away of the tape. When it was over, the pain had already faded and all that she felt was a tingling on the affected skin.

Mollie asked, "Do you need a bikini wax?"

"Not today," Andi managed to say, and bolted out of the cubicle.

Chapter 18

Kathleen Brackenbury sat in her empty classroom correcting English Composition tests. She had a hard time concentrating on the students' papers. Her mind kept wandering. Kathleen was 57 years old, British, and widowed for the last four years. She tucked a strand of ash-blond hair tinged with gray behind one ear, pushed the glasses that had been riding down to the tip of her nose back onto the bridge, and looked at her watch. It was quarter to eight in the evening; the new student would be here in 15 minutes. She had better get on with her work.

Having corrected several more tests, she drifted off again. Her life had drastically changed since her husband's death. He had lectured at University and she had taught English, history and geography at a high school in Los Angeles. After dear Frederic had passed away, she couldn't bear to live in their house filled with his memory. At the same time she had been disenchanted with her job at the high school. She had credentials in mathematics as well and would have welcomed teaching a broader curriculum. It had always been her dream to be in charge of a boarding school, so when she was offered the post here, she had accepted. She wouldn't exactly be running the school, but at least it would be a teaching position at a boarding school where pupils were eager to acquire knowledge.

As it turned out, she was dealing with students whose top priority was to become models. They were only in her classroom in order to finish high school and did not hunger for knowledge. Sure, she was paid extremely well, but that could by no means compensate for her lack of fulfillment. Oh, what she could do with a place like Optimum House if given the chance!

Andi stood in the doorway looking in. She saw three rows of student desks with a computer screen on each. On the blackboard at the head of the classroom, written in large letters, was the announcement "History test on Monday, chapters 8 through 12." The teacher sat behind her desk next to the blackboard, a stack of papers in front of her. Andi cleared her throat, and the instructor was pulled out of her daydream.

"You must be Antoinette LeJeune. I'm Mrs. Brackenbury. Come in and sit down. One of the front desks will do."

"Thank you. And please call me Andi."

"I shall address you as Antoinette. I do not wish to use abbreviations."

Andi shrugged and said, "Daddy always called me Antoinette."

"Your father was right in doing so. Why give a child a name and then chop it up?" She continued, "I understand you wish to get tutored."

"Sure do."

"You are a high school graduate, correct?"

"Yes, ma'am."

Mrs. Brackenbury asked, "Are you planning to attend college?"

"Someday, yes."

"What subject would you like me to tutor you in?"

"Cal-cluss."

"Sorry, dear, I don't seem to catch your diction."

Andi stared at the woman.

"What I mean is, I don't understand your accent."

"I have the same problem!"

The British teacher burst out laughing.

Andi continued, "I've taken algebra and geometry, but I never had - -"

Mrs. Brackenbury interrupted, "Oh, of course! You said calculus!"

"That's right."

"Why calculus?"

Andi reflected. Nothing seemed simple with this lady. She wasn't satisfied with being asked to teach her calculus; she wanted to know why!

Aloud she stated, "I like math."

Kathleen studied Andi's face intently. Then she asked, "Am I correct in assuming that you are attending this school because you wish to become a model?"

"That's right."

"Yet you aspire to further your mathematical education?"

"Well, ma'am, I look at it this way: There's no guarantee that I'll ever become a model, and even if I make it, the career won't last long."

The teacher smiled and remarked, "You are a practical young woman, Antoinette! I shall certainly tutor you in calculus."

"Great!"

"It will have to be in the evenings because we have conflicting schedules during the day."

"Evening is fine with me."

Then Mrs. Brackenbury said, "Mrs. Camden informed me that you anticipated private tutoring, but would you mind if another student joined us?"

Surprised, Andi asked, "There is another modeling student taking calculus?"

"Not yet, and he is not in the modeling class. The boy's name is Troy Hesselman."

"I don't understand."

"Let me explain. Troy is a health-program client. He is 15 and extremely smart, attending my academic class which is geared to 11th-and 12th-grade high school students. As I said, the boy is intelligent and has skipped grades along the way. He is mostly bored during class, especially in mathematic. I feel sorry for the lad; he doesn't fit in with his fellow clients and he has nothing in common with the aspiring models. So just now, when you told me you wish to be tutored in calculus, I thought that Troy could attend too. I shall tell him that this will excuse him from his regular math class, which surely should make his day."

Andi said, "I don't mind if we get tutored together."

"I will speak to him about the matter. The boy will welcome the proposal, I'm certain." And she added, "Would two evenings a week suit you?"

"Fine by me."

Then Mrs. Brackenbury said, "Today is Thursday. We will begin on Monday." And with a little smirk she stated, "That way, I shall have time to brush up on calculus, having not taught it in ages!"

Andi walked out of the classroom and mused, couldn't find a way to bring up the thefts. This woman is hard to tackle, but I'll think of something, come Monday.

Chapter 19

Andi had made it her routine to take an early-morning walk around the grounds. This gave her time to mull over the case. She also liked to shower first before giving Cyrilla a chance to hog the bathroom. Her roommate took 20-minute showers and then spent another eternity in the bathroom.

On this Friday of her first week at Optimum House, she grabbed a quick bite of breakfast in the dining hall and then exited the building through the east-wing side door. The early morning was crisp and chilly and Andi was glad she'd donned her hooded sweat jacket. Except for occasional chirping of birds, there was complete silence all around her. She took the path leading along the putting green. There was no one practicing at the moment.

The day before, she had seen Mr. Camden perfecting his putting skills and had stopped to chat with him for a minute. He'd remarked that putters and balls were kept in the small shed next to the green and that anyone was welcome to use the equipment. He had mentioned that the putters in the shed were standard "off the shelf" inexpensive putters and were flat on both sides, so that either a right-hander or lefty could use any of them. With a grin, he had added that obviously he would never leave his own personal putter in the shed with the others, as he didn't want anyone else to use it. Mr. Camden must have seen her ignorance about golf reflected in her eyes because he proudly described the advantages of his own personal putter that he was using for practice. He informed her that it was a mallet style putter custom-made for him, slightly heavier and longer to accommodate his height. Also, he pointed out that the face of his putter was grooved in the center, which allowed for a truer roll to the golf ball when struck.

Andi passed the putting green and hiked toward a plateau that she had explored on previous excursions. The elevated plain was a charmingly rustic spot for people to hike up to, sit on the wooden bench erected on its brink, and enjoy the magnificent view to the lake. There were two ways to arrive at the small clearing; one was through the woods, the other along open meadows. On this Friday, she chose to trek through the woods. The dirt path was moist with morning dew and slippery in spots.

Andi thought about the disturbing stuff that had happened. The thing with the dolls especially puzzled her. Early in the week she'd stopped at the display case in the hallway. The Barbie dolls were neatly arranged according to theme. She'd noticed a particular Barbie sitting on a swing, looking up at a Ken doll. She had had a gut feeling that these must have been the two dolls that were found lynched, even though the scene now looked serene again.

Although the woodsy area stretched over a relatively short distance, Andi suddenly panicked. She felt hemmed in by the tall pine trees blocking the sunlight. They appeared menacing and threatening to her. The absurd sensation that she was trapped in a vast forest with no way out overcame her. She quickened her step almost to a run. When she got to the clearing, she sighed with relief and stood still. What was that all about, she wondered. Is this place getting to me? Now, standing in the open grassland with the sun warming her face, she found her former anxiety unwarranted.

She kept to the left of the path and knew that in a short, steep climb she'd have reached her destination: the natural terrace in the clearing with the wooden bench on its rim.

Chapter 20

The boy noticed Andi's approach from his position on the bench.

Andi looked up and said, "Hi there! You've beat me to my favorite spot."

Then she reached the plateau and, flopping down next to him, went on, "I'm Andi. And what's your name?"

"Troy."

She looked downward to the lake and proclaimed, "What a glorious view!"

"I guess so," he replied.

"So you're not here to look at the scenery, then?"

He shook his head. Then he said, "You're a new student. I saw you in the dining hall."

"Yep. And I noticed you sitting at the health-program table. Must be hard to be thrown together with old folks."

He didn't answer and kept up his sullen expression.

Andi said, "You're not happy here, are you?"

"I hate this place!"

"Tell me about it."

"I don't know what's worse, the other clients or the school."

"You're 15, correct?"

"How did you know?"

"Mrs. Brackenbury told me."

He said, "I guess Brackenbury's okay, but the high school girls are airheads. I can't stand them."

"Are you making progress, though?"

"If you mean the weight, sure, I'm losing. I'll gain it all back when I'm home again, though. My parents think they're doing me a favor by sticking me in this madhouse, but they're wrong. Being fat is in our genes. Mom and Dad are overweight, just like most of my relatives."

"Are you an only child?"

"Yeah."

"Why do you think your parents want you to slim down?"

"They want me to have a better social life, is how they put it." And he added, "Fat or thin, I'll never fit in with kids my age. I'm not interested in sports or any of their heroes."

Andi asked, "What are you interested in?"

"Science. I want to become a scientist."

"You're a lucky guy, Troy. Most kids your age have no clue where they're headed."

"Maybe." Then he gave her a scrutinizing look and said, "Are you sure you want to be a model?"

Andi answered, "Why not? I'm 5'8 ¾" tall, not a giant among models, but okay." Then she turned her face sideways, pointed at her profile and said, "And look at these cheekbones!"

"That's not what I meant. You're not the type."

"Oh, really?"

"For one thing, I saw you driving up on a Harley-Davidson."

"Maybe I can't afford a car."

"But you're rich enough to pay for the modeling school?"

Andi thought that she'd better be careful with this boy. He was too damn smart. She couldn't just say whatever popped into her head.

Aloud she remarked, "Okay, so I enjoy riding a bike, but that doesn't mean I'm not modeling material."

He shrugged.

Then she asked, "So why did you come up here?"

After a pause he answered, "To think of Lupe."

"Who's Lupe?"

"The only friend I had here, and now she's dead."

Perplexed, Andi said, "She died?"

"Yeah, drowned in the pool."

"Wanna talk about her?"

Troy didn't respond, so Andi said, "You don't have to."

"I do want to tell you about Lupe." And he began to unburden himself. "We met up here every Friday on her day off. She was one of the maids. She only planned to work for two seasons and was saving up her money for a college education. Sometimes we played games, but mostly we just gabbed. Lupe was smart, and we talked about all kind of things."

He smiled and continued, "She wasn't afraid of Mrs. Garcia either. When the 'general' told her she wasn't supposed to mix with us inmates, Lupe set her straight and said that what she did and who she talked to on her day off was no one's business."

Andi said, "The 'general' is the head housekeeper in charge of the domestics?"

"Uh-huh. Lupe and I had nicknames for everybody and everything in this place. Mrs. Camden was the Pope; Mr. Camden, the disciple; Mrs. Demitris, the prototype; Mrs. Brackenbury, the Brit; Ms. Dugat, the court taster; and Mr. Jimenez, the stew. The modeling school students were the bimbos; the health-program clients, the inmates; and the patrons we called the tin gods."

Andi chuckled but immediately got serious again and asked, "When did Lupe drown?"

"Ten days ago. Her funeral was last Saturday. Except for Mr. and Mrs. Camden, there wasn't a soul there from Optimum House."

"Were you?"

"Sure. I asked my parents to take me. They always pick me up on Saturday mornings and then I spend the weekend at home. It's not far; we live in San Diego."

"So there weren't many people at Lupe's funeral?"

"Tons; she had lots of friends and relatives. Her parents were there." His eyes got moist as he continued, "I went over to them after the service. They didn't speak much English and we just hugged."

Andi inquired, "What happened? Why did she drown?"

"I heard she was cleaning the pool area and fell in. I guess she didn't know how to swim."

"Wasn't there anyone around to jump in and help her?"

"It happened early in the morning and she was alone."

"Did you know that she couldn't swim?"

Troy replied, "No, I didn't. We never talked about the pool or swimming."

And after a pause he added, "Someone must have known, though."

"What do you mean?"

"You know what I mean. You may become a model, but you're no dummy."

Andi gave him a long look. Then she said, "Troy, if you know something, come out with it. Your knowledge can put you in danger."

"I don't know anything," he answered. Then he asked, "What time is it?"

Andi glanced at her watch and replied, "7:35."

The boy jumped to his feet and said, "Class starts in 10 minutes; I'll be late!" and awkwardly ran down the short slope.

Chapter 21

To prove that she had nothing to fear, Andi purposely chose to walk through the woods once more on her way down to the house. The stately pine trees held no menace any longer and her earlier panic seemed silly now. She was thinking of Daddy and how he had eased her worries and fears by singing to her when she was a little girl. Smiling to herself, she started to whistle a little Cajun tune.

She was halfway down the path when a tall and lanky man appeared out of nowhere. He wore his hair in a crew cut, had aristocratic features, and appeared to be in his forties. Taken by surprise, Andi stopped whistling, and before she had a chance to say a word, he put his index finger in front of his mouth in a silencing gesture. She noticed his delicate hand and fingers with well-kept nails and thought, could this be the surgeon? Then he pointed upward to a nearby Douglas fir. Andi looked in the direction of his outstretched arm and spotted a small bird perched on a branch about 15 feet away. The man offered her his binoculars, and when she had located the tiny creature, she gazed at the magnified view of him. His body was brownish-buff and would otherwise have seemed inconspicuous except for a bright yellow stripe tinged with red on its head. How pretty, she mused, and then in a flash it flew off.

"What kind of bird was that?" Andi asked, as she handed the binoculars back.

"A golden-crowned kinglet," he replied. "It was a male. The female's crest is yellow with no red highlights."

"That's a big name for a small critter!" Then she

introduced herself and said, "Are you by chance Dr. Ronnquist?"

"That's correct."

"You've picked an interesting hobby! What kind of birds do you find in this area, then?"

"If you're really interested, I'll tell you."

"Sure am!"

So Brant Ronnquist began, "There are a large variety of birds to be found in the Big Bear area. One of the more dramatic birds is the handsome black-crowned Steller's jay with its distinctive black back and crown, and bright blue plumage. It's a fairly large bird, as is the acorn woodpecker, another native to these parts. It's easy to tell the male and female apart, as the male has a red cap extending back from a white forehead, while the female's red cap is smaller, located at the back of the head separated from a white forehead by a line of black feathers."

He paused, apparently trying to gauge Andi's interest. When she nodded, he went on, "Another extremely interesting bird is the osprey, an eagle-like creature, somewhat uncommon, but he lives near bodies of water. So Big Bear Lake is an ideal area for this bird as he has plenty of fish to catch. Ospreys are quite good 'fishermen,' and I was privileged to witness a kill through my binoculars the other day. The bird spotted a fish and made a dramatic dive from a height of about 50 feet and plunged feet first into the water after his prey."

Andi was just beginning to wonder if this lecture was going to include a description of every winged creature in Southern California when he suddenly stopped, grabbed her arm and whispered, "Quiet! I think you're about to have a real bird-watching treat! Walk ten paces to your right, take my binoculars and look midway up that small scrub pine, just beyond the hedgerow. Move slowly or you'll scare her off."

Andi did as he said, thinking, this could be exciting! Initially, she had feigned interest in the birds just to get the doctor talking, but now she was drawn into the adventure.

Through the glasses she saw an attractive bright yellow bird, no more than a few feet away. Ronnquist quietly moved nearer to her and under his breath said, "That, my dear young lady, is the female summer tanager! And where the female is, the male cannot be far away." He stepped out onto a small ridge and scanned the treetops. Sure enough, he pointed out a bright red bird, which apparently was the mate of the little yellow bird that had landed nearby.

Andi refocused the binoculars to get a closer look. He did have beautifully red plumage as well as a fairly large yellow beak, and seemed almost tame when he flew down closer to them as if to check out these humans.

Dr. Ronnquist triumphantly proclaimed, "You can tell everyone you know that you've seen the only entirely red bird in all of North America!"

"Oh, c'mon," Andi joshed. "Seems to me that the cardinal is also red."

"Ah, yes, but the cardinal has a tuft of black feathers around its eyes and beak, so there!" he retorted playfully. He continued, "You might also find it interesting that these particular tanagers are considered to be wasp and bee specialists, as those insects are a major part of their diet. The bird catches a bee in flight and kills it by beating it against a branch. Before eating the bee, the tanager removes the stinger by rubbing it on a branch. And voila, a tasty meal!"

Andi replied with genuine amazement, "Well, sir, sure thing you've got me hooked on learning more about your feathered creatures."

Now that the conversation had reverted to normal tones, the tanager pair, perhaps disturbed by their voices, flew off together.

The good doctor watched their departure and said, "You know, I've made friends with a summer tanager who greets me regularly up on the clearing. I've named him Eddie, and I think he may have followed me down here. But this is the first time I've seen his girlfriend."

They then walked down the trail together, and as they came within a short distance of the house, Andi said, "I heard that someone swiped your binoculars off the entrance chest in the dining hall."

"Yes, that was at the beginning of my stay here. What a nerve! Even though I have another pair of binoculars, the ones that were taken are my favorites. I got them back, however, I'm glad to say."

"What do you make of the other thefts and pranks that have happened since?"

The doctor shrugged. "I haven't really thought about it. It's no concern of mine," he said.

Chapter 22

Emma Demitris said, "All right, class, this concludes our first week of posture and runway training. We'll get back to more of it later in the session. With the exception of Cyrilla Washington, all of you need to improve your walk. I suggest you practice every day. Next week, we'll focus on facial expression and makeup application. On Tuesday, our makeup artist will pay us a visit. Bring your cases to class, but don't wear any kind of makeup."

Susie had her hand raised continuously during Emma's speech, so the principal finally said, "What is it, Susie?"

"May we use the runway classroom to practice?"

"You may. The room is never locked. However, you don't need a runway to polish your walk. Drill your stride to perfection when you stroll down the hall, in and out of a room; in short, everywhere you go."

Emma turned back to the rest of the students and asked, "Anything else?" She got no response and announced, "Class dismissed."

As the aspiring models scampered out the door, she said, "Just a moment, Andi. I didn't want to embarrass you in front of the class, but - -" Andi held her breath, thinking, shit, I've blown my cover! - - "get yourself a new pair of pumps. Your right heel looks like it was chewed up by a dog."

"Yes, ma'am," Andi replied, exhaling with relief.

Minutes later, she was in her room changing. Stripped down to her bra and panties when Cyrilla came out of the bathroom, she said, "I'm taking a dark load to the laundry room. Wanna add some of your clothes?"

Cyrilla replied, "How sweet of you! Yes, I have some laundry to do." Then she glanced at Andi and said, "What *are* you wearing?"

"Underwear. What's it look like to you?"

"Ugly!" Cyrilla shuddered.

"Who cares? It's clean and no one sees it."

"I see it, you see it, and who knows, this weekend someone else might see it!"

Andi laughed.

"Girl! Don't you like to feel pretty all over? It's time I take you to What's-her-name's Secret! Are you free tomorrow?"

"Sure thing. I need to buy some new pumps anyway."

"Then let's go to the mall. From what I've seen you've got hanging in the closet, you need a whole new wardrobe, and I've been meaning to buy a frame. Nancy drew a picture of me, and I wanna send it to Granny."

Chapter 23

Saturday morning Andi said, "I've got my goggles back, so let's take the bike."

Cyrilla grimaced and replied, "Don't jive me, girl!"

"I think you'd like straddling the Harley. It's fun," Andi teased.

"Get real. A motorcycle is not on my list of things I aim to straddle! Besides, we'll need room for all the stuff we buy."

As they walked toward Cyrilla's fire-red Mazda in the parking lot, Andi asked, "Don't we have to sign out?"

"Sign out?"

"Tell Mrs. Camden we're leaving the campus."

"This here is a modeling school, not a prison!"

"I just figured there'd be some kind of rules since most students are minors."

Cyrilla said, "I never thought about it. I guess Mrs. Camden keeps track of the kids on weekends. There may even be a curfew for them during the week. After all, she has a responsibility to their parents." She smiled and added, "You and I can come and go as we please."

They got into the car, and while turning the ignition key, Cyrilla said, "We could shop at Big Bear, but let's drive down to the Redlands mall."

"Okay by me."

Neither of them spoke for a long stretch on the way down to the flatland. They were driving a different route than Andi had taken when she first came to Optimum House. Highway 38 took them through Big Bear City and on a 50-mile ride all the way down to Redlands. After leaving Big Bear behind, the road climbed even higher through the vast pine forest, until it reached the summit of 8400 feet. Then the steady descent began.

Andi broke the silence and asked, "So most people leave on weekends?"

"Depends how far away they live. Parents pick some of the kids up; others just stay put or drive somewhere if they have a car. I don't really know the high school students, but out of our little group, only Nancy goes home to her momma regularly. Susie lives in San Francisco, so she hangs around or visits friends. Olivia is gone every weekend. I have no clue where she goes, but come Mondays we have to listen to stories about her love life."

"How about you?"

"Came to the school straight from Georgia and haven't got a home in California yet." She added, "No problem finding a way to pass my free time, though!"

They had finally arrived at the lowland. Andi gazed at the scenery. She noticed carpets of yellow wildflowers growing along the sides of the road and next to the riverbank on their left, as well as all over the hillside to the right. Never seen anything like this in Louisiana, she marveled.

As they were driving into the outskirts of Redlands, Andi asked, "Your runway walk really comes to you naturally?"

Cyrilla laughed and answered, "That's what everyone thinks, including Mrs. Demitris! I'll tell you a secret. I've been practicing ever since I was nine and saw a fashion show on TV!"

The two young women got out of the Mazda at the mall parking lot, and Cyrilla asked, "Are you ready for shopping?"

"Sure am," Andi replied, not yet knowing that shopping with Cyrilla gave the word a new meaning. Andi was used to going into a store, looking for the item she needed, buying it, and then leaving.

Cyrilla suggested, "Let's do lingerie first while we're still fresh."

All heads were literally turning and eyes focused on Cyrilla as they sauntered through the mall. Besides the strikingly attractive face, she had that proud, majestic stride.

She suddenly let out an audible laugh and said, "There they go again, staring at the tall black girl."

"No, they're gawking at the African American goddess!"

"Ain't you sweet!"

When they entered the intimate apparel store, Andi headed directly toward the panties rack. Her friend held her back and made her stop to admire a negligee and dressing gown set. Then Cyrilla gave her a tour of the place, touching numerous garments and commenting on their merits. The store manager couldn't have done a better job. When at last they ambled toward the underwear, Andi had forgotten the reason for being there. Then the real shopping began.

Cyrilla had talked her in and out of several pairs of different panties and made her try on numerous bras. She also insisted that Andi needed new nightwear. Then it was Cyrilla's turn to try on bathing suits. She took forever changing, and then came out of the try-on-room modeling each suit for Andi, seeking her opinion.

They stopped to have a bite to eat, and after lunch their shopping spree continued. When they returned to the car in the early evening, Andi had purchased a new pair of black pumps, two dresses, pajamas, three bras and six pairs of underwear. Cyrilla took home several new outfits, a swimsuit and a wooden picture frame.

On the drive back Cyrilla asked, "Had fun?"

"Yeah, but I'm beat. Never reckoned shopping was this much work!"

Chapter 24

Jeffrey lay awake. Normally he would fall asleep soon after lovemaking with Iris, but not on that Saturday night. It was clear that the sex had satisfied them both. So why couldn't he ban the suspicion from his mind? Because Chad Richmond had arrived that day, that's why. After returning from the Maui vacation, he told himself that he'd imagined it all. Now, with Chad here, his mistrust was back.

He had always known that Iris had a magnetizing effect on men; however, that fact had never bothered him in the past. He was proud to have a spouse whom people admired, but that had changed when they met Chad in Hawaii. In the beginning he was glad that the man asked Iris to dance. She loved dancing and he wanted her to have fun. It wasn't her fault that she had a cripple for a husband. Golf was the only sport left for him to pursue since the knee injury. So he had welcomed Chad's offer to show Iris around the island while he pursued his golfing.

When and why he first suspected that the two were having an affair, he couldn't say. Once the notion had entered his head, he wasn't able to shake it from his mind. And could he really blame her? She had married an able-bodied football hero, not a limping fool. Yet he had always thought she loved him. He surely was crazy for her and would do anything she asked.

The moonlight illuminated part of the bedroom, and he could see Iris clearly. She had been sleeping like a baby for the last hour. He knew that the most important thing in Iris's life was the success of Optimum House. Now she worried about the bizarre incidents. The assumption that someone was out to ruin her precious business was absurd.

Jeffrey's last thought before he finally lost consciousness was, I wonder if Andi is any good at detecting?

Chapter 25

On Sunday morning, Andi felt it was high time that she took the Harley for a spin. She had the entire day to herself, so she planned to explore the south shore of the lake. She couldn't have picked a better day; not a cloud in the sky and the predicted local temperatures were in the mid-seventies. She rode out of the driveway and turned right into Highway 38. What a lovely place, she mused as she surveyed the landscape.

Near Bear Valley Dam, picturesque old cabins sat on giant rock formations among pine trees. A short distance away was Garstin Island, formed from nothing but boulders. On top of the rock, charming Oriental-style houses built in the early 1900s commanded the attention of tourists and locals alike.

When Andi reached the dam area where the lake ended and came to a point, she kept to the left. She was now on Highway 18 and riding parallel with the south shore. Soon the road ascended slightly and wound around narrow curves. Andi loved to ride out each bend, her body in tune with the bike. Then the highway eased into a short downgrade before it leveled out and remained straight, all the way to Big Bear Lake.

The center of town was simply called The Village. Andi came to a fork in the road. Staying on Highway 18 would guide her along the lake, while turning right into Village Drive would take her into the heart of The Village. She chose Village Drive, turned up an alley and parked the Harley in a lot framed by tall pine trees.

She was not alone on her stroll around The Village; the place was crowded with tourists. Andi had never been to

Europe, but glancing at the storefronts of the charming mountain town, she imagined that villages in the Alps looked like this. She browsed in the quaint shops on Village Drive and along cross streets, most of them mom-and-pop enterprises. Although the town was geared toward tourism, there was an atmosphere of warmth and old-fashioned hospitality.

Andi was window shopping, occasionally going into a store that caught her interest. She smelled food when she walked by a bistro with outdoor seating and suddenly realized that she was starving. There were a variety of restaurants to choose from. She settled for a grill and then ordered a cheeseburger with everything on it, French fries, and a large Coke. The heck with Ms. Dugat's maintenance diet, she thought with a grin.

Thus satisfied, she ambled down Pine Knot Avenue in the direction of the lake. At the marina folks could cruise the lake in a pontoon boat accommodating up to 12 people. Rental equipment for various activities was also offered, including water skiing, wake boarding, wave runners and outboard fishing boats. It seemed too early in the season for water sports, but Andi noticed a fishing vessel leaving the marina.

She strolled over to the rental office and asked the attendant, "Sir, what kind of fish do you catch in your lake?"

The young man smiled and replied, "I don't catch any. I'm a vegan."

"What's that?"

"I don't eat any animal products."

"Oh." Then she thought about it and said, "But you rent out boats for fishing?"

"I don't own the place. I just work here."

Then he gave her an appraising glance and asked, "May I buy you a drink after I get off work?"

"No thanks, I don't drink with vegans." And she continued, "So what kind of fish do other folks catch here?"

"Rainbow trout, bass, catfish or panfish," he answered testily.

Andi gave him a dazzling smile, saying, "Thank you for the information," and moved on, continuing her walk along the shore.

She decided on taking a different route on her way back, riding around the lake and getting "home" from the opposite direction. So she continued east on Highway 18 and after about four or five miles was riding through Big Bear City, situated at the end of the lake. Not much of a city, she thought, despite the fact that she had crossed a road which led to Big Bear City Airport a moment earlier. Soon she was turning left onto Highway 38, which landed her back at the north shore.

Andi was riding along North Shore Drive when she saw a little white convertible with its top down coming out of a driveway and turning into the road ahead of her. She glimpsed someone with a mop of ash-blond hair in the driver's seat before the car went around a curve and out of sight. No mistaking that hair; that was Olivia! I wonder what she's up to? Andi thought, and promptly rode up the driveway.

Only a few cars were parked in the large lot in front of St. Joseph's Catholic Church. Andi stared at the building and then suddenly laughed out loud, thinking, Olivia must have stopped by to confess all of her weekend sins.

Chapter 26

Chad Richmond took the last few steps on his hike up to the natural terrace where Iris sat waiting for him on the wooden bench.

"Alone at last!" he exclaimed, and rushed to embrace her.

Iris held up a hand in protest and stopped him, saying, "Not here! There's a patron running around with binoculars."

Baffled, Chad asked, "Then where?"

She stated calmly, "Now Chad, I told you that we have to be careful. I still think it's a bad idea for you to be here. You're lucky Jeffrey drove away to play golf, or I wouldn't have agreed to meet you up here."

"Can you sneak out at night?"

"I doubt it."

He burst out, "I have to be near you. Please give me another chance."

She did not respond.

He grabbed both her hands, and holding them in his, declared, "I love you, Iris."

She pulled away and said gently, "Get a hold of yourself, Chad. You behave like a lovesick schoolboy."

"You marched to a different drummer in Hawaii."

"That was then. There is too much at stake for me here."

He exploded, "Don't tell me you love Jeffrey!"

She looked him in the eye and replied, "I always have." And after a pause she said, "I have to go now. Wait a few minutes before you start down."

She was already on her descent when Chad hollered after her, "When shall I see you again?"

Iris turned around and answered, "At dinner, like everyone else."

Trekking toward the house she thought, Chad is getting to be a problem. How on earth did I let myself get involved with him?

Chapter 27

Andi peeked into the gym on Monday morning and saw a few health-program clients working out on a variety of equipment. They used treadmills, Stairmasters, stationary bicycles and so forth. Mr. Camden assisted a middle-aged woman with her weight training. So Andi walked over to a row of bicycles, hopped on the nearest one, and started peddling. The gentleman riding the bike next to her was out of breath and soaked in sweat. She glanced at him. He was about 40 with a full baby face and a well-rounded body to match.

He suddenly stopped the bicycle. When his heartbeat stabilized, he turned to Andi and said, "Hi there! My name is Roland Wempel."

"I'm Andi LeJeune."

"You must be a new student. We already met in front of Ms. Dugat's office the other day."

"I remember."

He pointed at his belly and said, "You obviously know why I'm here." And grinning he added, "I've lost 35 pounds already and have only 50 more to go."

Andi gave him a thumb's up while continuing her frantic peddling.

When he smiled, dimples appeared on each cheek. He asked, "Are you the one whose goggles were snatched?"

"That's me! I got them back, though."

He chuckled and said, "I know. I'd have liked to see the face on that pompous ass, Applebee, when he found them in his breakfast!"

"You don't like him?"

"I don't know him, but he's the most unsociable person I've ever met. He doesn't acknowledge anyone around him, except Mrs. Camden."

Andi led the conversation back to the matter at hand and said, "I heard about the strange happenings here. Was something stolen from you?"

"No, but someone stuck a makeup case into my backpack." He cackled, "It was funny. We were on a nature walk and, reaching for my trail mix, I pulled out makeup instead."

"Are you worried about what's going on?"

He thought about it and then replied, "No, but I'm starting to get annoyed. I mean, enough is enough! Whoever is pulling these stunts should give it a rest."

Andi nodded.

He said, "Here comes Paula! I'm leaving. She gives me a headache with her chatter." He stepped off the bike and whispered, "Be careful what you tell her. That woman is a walking encyclopedia."

Paula Parsall walked toward the vacated bike next to Andi and climbed on it awkwardly. Then she remarked, "Roland dodges me like the plague. I wonder what he's got to hide?" Without taking a breath between sentences, she continued, "You look lovely on a bicycle, my dear!"

"Thank you!"

Then Paula concentrated on exercising and grew silent. Her short legs attacked the pedals with vigor. She was not severely overweight, about 20 pounds at most. Brown, curly hair framed her chubby face, and her dark sparkling eyes belied the fact that she was already in her forties.

She soon tired and had to ride at a slower pace, and then gave up altogether. Andi also quit. *Live the role,* she thought. Don't build up those calf muscles.

Paula remarked, "I enjoyed the chat we had the other day. Did you say you had a boyfriend?"

"I don't remember saying so," Andi replied.

"Well, do you?"

"Maybe." And she added, "Do you?"

Paula laughed heartily and stated, "Aren't you the cautious one! To answer your question, no, I don't. My husband wouldn't like it."

Andi smiled and said, "Husbands generally don't!" Then she asked, "What do you make of the weird stuff that's been going on?"

"I don't like it. Someone among us is off his or her rocker."

"Do you have a hunch as to who?"

"Believe me, I've been trying to figure it out, but I'm getting nowhere."

Jeffrey walked over to them and said, "Your turn, Paula."

"Shucks," she retorted, "I thought I could sneak out today!" She got off the bike and followed her trainer to the weights.

Andi lingered idly on her bicycle and did some serious thinking. She had no idea how much time had elapsed when she was abruptly jolted out of her reverie.

"A penny for your thoughts," said Jeffrey, standing next to her.

She jumped. "Oh, Mr. Camden!"

"Sorry, I didn't mean to startle you."

Andi looked at her watch and said, "Oh, good. It's only 9:25. I've got plenty of time to change before class starts. Mrs. Demitris doesn't put up with tardiness."

"I can imagine!"

Then Andi looked at him intently and said, "You don't like her, do you?"

"What makes you think that?"

"I was right behind you the other morning, when you walked down to the house from the putting green. You saw Mrs. Demitris coming along the path from the opposite direction. So you deliberately went around the long way through the pool area instead of straight ahead to the side door."

"You are observant, Andi!"

"I noticed you avoided her on other occasions too."

He said, "I didn't realize that it's that obvious. Actually, I don't dislike Emma. I feel uncomfortable around her, that's all."

"Oh?"

"All right, Andi, I'll tell you. A long time ago I dated Emma. She and Iris were roommates. One day I met Iris when I picked Emma up at their apartment. I fell in love with Iris at first sight."

"So you dumped Mrs. Demitris."

"Yes."

"But, Mr. Camden, that must've been ages ago!"

"Twelve years." He went on, "I treated Emma badly at the time. This must sound silly to you, but I still feel guilty. Emma seems to have forgiven me a long time ago, and the two women are getting along just fine. Still, I can't help feeling uneasy around her."

"I hear you."

He looked around. There wasn't another soul left in the gym, so he asked, "How is the investigation coming along?"

Andi considered the question for several seconds before answering, "I'm working on it."

Chapter 28

At dinner that evening, Andi was sitting at the students' table with her peers. They were having rainbow trout, little red potatoes, and asparagus. The meal tasted yummy. Again, she was amazed at what the cook could do in spite of Ms. Dugat's orders.

Susie turned to Andi and said, "I'm so excited about tomorrow; I can hardly wait!"

"What happens tomorrow?"

"Don't be daft! The makeup artist is coming."

"Yes, of course. I'm tickled to death!"

"Don't forget to bring your makeup case to class."

Then Andi looked over to the patrons' table. Mrs. Camden seemed surrounded by admirers. The first lady of Optimum House sat between Adam Applebee and Valencia Kirkland. The man seated on the other side of the actress must be the new patron, Chad Richmond, Andi thought. His hair was dark and he had classic good looks, from what she could glean across the room. Mr. Camden and Dr. Ronnquist had their backs turned to her, so she couldn't see their faces. The ones she did see, however, appeared to be gazing at their hostess, spellbound. She'd only seen Mr. Applebee once before at dinner. He apparently preferred eating in his room. She had heard of the famous writer but had never read any of his books. He looked ordinary, with light brown hair balding at the crown. He had a pallid complexion, consistent with someone who avoided the outdoors.

Olivia was eying the patrons' corner too and blurted, "Isn't the new guy a dream? I'd like to jump his bones!"

Cyrilla commented, "You're after every guy's bones, Olivia. So get a grip!"

Some of the younger students giggled.

Olivia seemed to enjoy her audience and yelled to the shy artist sitting at the end of the table, "Hey, Nancy! Draw me a picture of the new patron!"

Nancy ignored her and seemed preoccupied with the food in her plate. Everyone at the table fell silent as well. For a while, the only voices audible came from other groups in the dining hall.

Then Andi addressed Susie, "What do you think about the strange things going on in this place?"

"What do you mean?"

"You know, the stealing and stuff."

Susie said, "Oh, that! I guess there's a kleptomaniac running loose."

"Was anything taken from you?"

"Not yet. I've been lucky, I guess." She added, "Whoever is doing it sure got to you in a hurry."

Andi nodded. "Yep, the minute I had my foot in the door!"

Chapter 29

At a quarter to nine on Tuesday morning, Huber was unlocking the door to her office when the phone rang.

She hurried to her desk and picked up the receiver, saying, "Good morning! R.A. Huber. How can I help you?"

"Hi, Mrs. Huber, it's Andi."

"Well, hello! So what's new since your last report?"

"I was in the torture chamber and I also got my goggles back."

"What torture chamber?"

"Got my eyebrows waxed."

Huber laughed and then said, "You know that once you start waxing, you'll have to keep doing it."

"No, ma'am. After I leave here I'll let them grow wild again."

"So where did your goggles show up?"

"In Adam Applebee's breakfast. Mrs. Camden called me to her office and gave them back to me, so I picked her brain about a couple of other things."

"Such as?"

"I asked her to tell me about each theft and the other happenings in the right order. She came up with lots of info. What she couldn't remember, I got from other people. I wrote it all down, so I'll read from my list.

"Number one: Dr. Ronnquist's binoculars swiped from dining hall entrance chest. Found by cook in kitchen cupboard. Number two: Mrs. Demitris's alarm clock taken from her room while asleep. Found in Paula Parsall's room sitting on scale. By the way, she thought that placing the alarm on her scale was a joke in poor taste. Number three: Barbie and Ken discovered lynched in the showcase by Nancy Zagarian. Number four: Olivia's makeup case disappeared from downstairs bathroom. Turned up in Roland Wempel's backpack. Number - -"

Huber interrupted, "Slow down, please! I'm writing all this down."

"Oh, sorry. Where was I? Oh yeah, number five: Cyrilla's dress taken from laundry room. Found cut to shreds in wastebasket by maid. Number six: Tutor's grading list snatched from her briefcase during class intermission. Discovered in dining hall in a bouquet of flowers by Mrs. Garcia. Number seven: Valencia Kirkland's diamond bracelet stolen from sauna room. Recovered in Mrs. Camden's shoe. Number eight: My goggles lifted from administrative office. Served to Mr. Applebee on a plate for breakfast.

"Did you get all that, Mrs. Huber?"

"I think so. What's the other thing you learned from Mrs. Camden?"

"All the clients and patrons are here alone and they can't all be single. So I asked her if it was against policy for them to bring spouses and family. She answered that it wasn't, but that patrons usually wanted to get away from their everyday life and preferred to come alone. But if any of them chose to bring spouse and family, the suites were big enough to accommodate all. As for the clients, she said, they do a lot better alone than getting well-meaning pressure from their loved ones."

Andi went on, "I met a few more people since my last report. I ran into Dr. Ronnquist in the woods and had a long talk with him, mostly about his bird-watching hobby. I faked interest and actually ended up enjoying the lesson. He loves to watch his feathered friends and pays little attention to anything else. I talked with Valencia Kirkland. She's friendly enough, but self-centered. I like Roland Wempel, one of the clients. He warned me that Paula Parsall was a gossip, which I already knew from my earlier chats with her. I haven't met Adam Applebee yet. He's pretty much holed up in his room and only came to eat in the dining hall twice. From a distance, he looked colorless. The new patron, Chad Richmond, only got here last weekend, so I doubt he could tell me anything important. I haven't talked with the cook or the housekeeper. Can't think of a way to tackle either one since I'm a modeling school student and *living the role*."

Regula couldn't help but chuckle at Andi's last remark.

The young woman continued, "I had my first tutoring lesson yesterday evening. Mrs. Brackenbury is from England, and I don't always get what she says, but I think she's sharp. The woman is wasting her time here, and I reckon she'd be happier teaching in a prep school or something. I share the tutoring with Troy Hesselman. Let me tell you about Troy," she said, and related the conversation she had had with the boy.

Huber asked, "Do you think he knows something about the maid's accident?"

"I'm not sure."

"Try to bring the subject up with him again."

"Okay."

The lady detective declared, "You're doing really well, Andi!"

"There's more. I don't know if it means anything, but I'm sure that Iris Camden is bewitching some people."

Huber remarked, "So you feel that too! Tell me who's affected, if you can."

"Mr. Applebee, Ms. Kirkland, and her husband would jump through hoops for her, artificial knee and all. The new patron, Mr. Richmond, has got it badly too. The only patron that seems immune to her is Dr. Ronnquist."

"Are any of the modeling students or weight-loss clients drawn to her?"

Andi replied, "That isn't easy to figure out, since I hardly see them together. Could be that my roommate, Cyrilla, is hypnotized too, but I'm not sure."

"How about teachers and staff?"

"I think Mrs. Demitris admires her also. As for the others, I can't say. Haven't seen any of them in close contact with Mrs. Camden."

"I see."

Then Andi asked, "Did you know that Iris Camden and Emma Demitris were roommates at one time?"

"Mrs. Camden mentioned that they know one another from their modeling days, but I don't recall her saying anything about rooming together. How did you find that out?"

"Had another chat with Mr. Camden. He told me that he dated Mrs. Demitris first and met his wife through her."

"Interesting."

"Can you believe the man still feels guilty about dumping her twelve years ago?"

Huber remarked, "Sounds extreme." Then she inquired, "Anything else?"

"That's all I can think of right now."

"Keep up the good work, Andi. By the way, I hope you're not calling from your room unless you're positive your roommate is safely busy somewhere else."

"Don't worry, boss. I'm sitting on a bench above the woods with nothing but open meadows around me. There ain't a soul in sight!"

Chapter 30

When Andi went to her room to change before class, she heard the water running in the shower.

She stuck her head in the bathroom door and, raising her voice, asked, "May I use the toilet real quick?"

Cyrilla had her back turned to the glass shower door and yelled, "Be my guest."

On her way out Andi said, "You'd better hurry or you'll be late!"

"I'm not coming to class. I'm getting another allergy shot."

"See you tonight, then."

Andi was all the way down the long hall on the ground floor when she suddenly stopped and murmured, "Shit! I forgot the makeup." So she turned around, hurried up the stairs, and walked back to her room. Once inside, she rushed to the bathroom and flung the door open, then stopped paralyzed in the doorway and stared, her green eyes as wide as saucers.

Cyrilla stood in front of the mirror using an electric shaver on her face.

Andi finally found her voice and exclaimed, "You're a transvestite!"

"No, I'm a woman trapped in a man's body. There's a difference." And she added, "I'm sorry for shocking you. I've little facial hair, but I still need to shave once in a while. Soon that'll be taken care of, though."

Andi replied, "But there's something I don't understand. Why are you here?"

"Same as everyone else; I wanna be a model."

"There are classes for male students. So why the disguise?"

"I don't wanna be a male model. I'm a woman."

"Well, you sure fooled me. I had no idea! Wait a minute. The shots you're getting; they're not allergy shots. They're female hormones, right?"

Cyrilla nodded and shared, "And I'm getting a sex change operation as soon as the modeling class session is over. I'm seeing a psychologist, and she agrees that I'm basically a woman. I think and react like one."

Andi studied her and then said, "So you changed your name, came west, and enrolled in the school here."

"I changed the name a long time ago." She grinned and added, "No big jump from Cyrus Washington to Cyrilla Washington."

"When did you become Cyrilla?"

"The year I turned 14. By then, I was sure of my identity."

"So you've lived as a girl for over four years?"

"That's right."

Andi thought about this and then said, "The other kids must've made fun of you when you suddenly changed your gender."

"The transition was easy. Granny and I moved, so I was in a different school district."

Suddenly, Andi remembered the conversation they'd had when they first met and asked, "Did the settlement from your lawsuit have anything to do with sexual harassment?"

"Among other things."

Andi quickly said, "You don't have to tell me if you don't feel like it."

After a pause Cyrilla answered, "I want you to know."

Then she told her story. "I was walking home from school in my junior high year. Two young guys stopped their car next to me and got out. They said things like, 'Where are you going, tall beauty?' And, 'Don't be stuck up; talk to us!' I didn't answer, but I knew what they were after. I saw it in their eyes. I started running, but they caught up with me and threw me on the ground. I screamed and tried to fight them off, but I didn't stand a chance. Then they pulled up my dress and were about to rape me. When they ripped off my panties and found something unexpected, they flew into a rage and beat me until I lost consciousness."

"I'm sorry, Cyrilla."

She continued, "I had a broken arm, severe head wounds and a concussion. I woke up in the hospital two days later."

"Were they white guys?"

"What difference does it make? One was black, the other white. It wasn't a racial thing."

Andi inquired, "So they caught the bastards, and you filed suit for assault and attempted rape?"

"Something like that. But we settled out of court."

"Hell, why did you do that?"

"One of the punks had a rich daddy who hired a top-notch attorney. When they first made me a settlement offer, I said 'no way!' I wanted my day in court. Then the guy's lawyer made it clear that the case could turn real ugly for me at a trial."

"What did he mean by that?"

"The two scumbags claimed I was and looked like a whore, and that I lured and enticed them under false pretense. All lies, of course. I looked like and was a schoolgirl, walking home from school."

"So what were you afraid of? Even if they thought you were a hooker doesn't change that they attacked and beat you up."

Cyrilla sighed and then said, "Right, but that attorney would've dragged me through the mud and made a freak show of me. He'd have called Granny as a witness and would've made minced meat out of her. I couldn't bear to have Granny go through all that. Besides, you never know with a jury. I could have lost."

Andi nodded.

"So I accepted the huge settlement, and it'll pay for my surgery."

"Thanks for sharing this," Andi said. Then she asked, "Does anybody know your secret?"

"You're the only one, and I'd like to keep it that way."

"I won't tell, Cyrilla. I promise."

"Thank you."

Andi gazed at her friend and stated, "Yeah, you *are* a woman! And a beauty to boot!" Then she lowered her eyes and burst out, "Hold on a minute! I saw you in a swimsuit the other day. Nothing was showing. What did you do with your, eh, thing?"

Cyrilla stated, "You don't wanna know, but believe me, it was extremely painful." Then she looked at her watch and scolded, "*You're* the one who's late for class!"

Chapter 31

Peter and Regula were comfortably established in their recliners. They had watched the evening news, and now Peter began channel surfing.

He finally gave up and said, "There's nothing worth watching," and pushed the "off" button of the remote.

His spouse remarked, "Andi called this morning."

"Did she have news for you?"

"She read me a list of thefts and transgressions in chronological order. I wrote it all down, but left my notes in the office. After her call I studied the list at length, so it's all in my head. There were a total of eight incidents."

Peter said, "Tell me what's on the list." So Regula recounted the conversation in detail.

When she came to a stop, he asked. "Do you think the offenses were done at random, or is there a purpose?"

"I've been wondering about that. There appears to be no rhyme or reason behind the misdeeds. Yet there's got to be an objective, otherwise these acts make no sense."

"Unless we're dealing with a nut."

Regula responded, "The culprit is sane. I'm certain of that."

Then her husband said, "All three groups are represented in these offenses. What I mean is, you can't just concentrate on one lot, like the students, for instance."

"True. I scrutinized the list more than once, trying to find a common factor, but couldn't come up with one. Then I turned it around and asked myself, who is not involved?"

"I've lost you."

"The individuals not affected in any of the incidents, either as victims or persons of discovery, are Jeffrey Camden, Nadine Dugat, Susie Seales and Troy Hesselman."

Peter asked, "You think that's significant?"

"No, but I presume that the perpetrator would make sure he or she is involved in one way or another."

"Oh, I get it! The person doesn't want to be thought of as the exception."

"Exactly."

"Where is the display case with the dolls located?"

"On the ground floor hallway of the main building."

"Lots of foot traffic there, I imagine?"

Regula said, "I see what you're getting at, and you're correct. The corridor is a busy place all day long, and the culprit wouldn't dare set up the lynch scene with people passing by. That deed, like some others, must've been carried out at night."

"What else did Andi tell you?"

"That she met some more people. By the way, do you know Adam Applebee?"

"He was at the writer's convention in Geneva, but I didn't talk with him."

"Have you read any of his books?"

"No, but he seems to get good reviews. Why do you ask?"

"Just wondering what you thought of him. As a writer, that is."

"Sorry, I can't help you out."

Then she said, "Andi noticed that thing about Iris Camden too."

"What thing?"

"That it's as though she can cast a spell on people."

Peter laughed and asked, "Is Andi spellbound?"

"No, but apparently most of the patrons are."

"Interesting! Do you think that she uses this talent of hers to make people do things against their will?"

"Possibly."

"Getting back to the thefts and spiteful pranks, are you closer to figuring out the truth?"

She shook her head and after a long pause finally said, "I'm uneasy."

"Why?"

"I fear that these incidents are just a prelude of worse to come."

Chapter 32

At four in the afternoon on Wednesday, Andi walked out of her photo session. She was exhausted. *I had no idea having a picture taken could be so much work*, she thought. *That guy must've snapped a zillion shots until I got a cramp in my neck. I'd rather do hard labor!*

The library door stood open, so Andi peeked inside and saw Troy sitting at a table, absorbed in a book. The boy seemed captivated and detached from his surroundings. His freckled face, framed by reddish-blond hair in a mass of unruly curls, was pulled tight in concentration. He suddenly looked up.

Andi walked a few steps into the room and asked, "What're you reading?"

He took a second before he answered, "About quantum gravity."

"Oh, heady stuff!"

"Uh-huh."

"Wanna take a break and talk with me?"

He shrugged and replied, "Sure. What's up?"

Andi looked at him gravely and said, "I've been thinking over what you told me about your friend Lupe."

"Yeah?"

"What did you mean?"

"About what?"

"You said that someone must've known Lupe couldn't swim. What were you trying to tell me?"

He shrugged again.

"You suspect that someone pushed Lupe into the pool?"

"Maybe."

"Troy, what's on your mind?"

"Nothing." And he added, "I wouldn't tell you if I knew anything. Look what happened to Lupe!"

Andi was aware of the steady foot-traffic in the hallway as people passed by the open door, so she changed the subject and said, "Guess you'll have to go to class now?"

"Nope. There's only math left today. I can skip it since I'm taking calculus with you."

"So you're free for the rest of the day?"

"Yeah."

"I need a change of pace; the photographer gave me a headache. Come, I'll take you for a ride."

The boy's gray eyes widened, and he asked, "On the Harley-Davidson?"

"You bet!"

"Cool!"

"Get a jacket, and I'll meet you in the parking lot."

As Andi climbed the stairs, she thought, I knew Daddy's helmet would come in handy someday.

She took him to Big Bear Lake. They enjoyed each other's company, strolling through the quaint village. Andi didn't bring up the maid's drowning incident. She knew Troy well enough by now. Pressuring him was useless. If he was willing to share more, he'd do so in time.

As they ambled by a bakery, Andi said, "Let's have some sweets and skip Ms. Dugat's diet."

"Cool!"

They went inside the crowded shop and stood in line. Andi was debating whether to have a brownie or a chocolate chip cookie. She turned around to ask Troy what he'd like. The boy wasn't there. Suddenly alarmed, she quickly left the bakery.

She found him on the sidewalk and he looked like he was struggling to breathe.

She rushed over to him yelling, "What happened?"

When he had recovered enough to talk, he stuttered, "Smelled peanuts in there."

"You're allergic to peanuts?"

"Highly."

"Do you need medical help?"

"I'll be fine in a few minutes, I think."

"Let's sit down someplace, then."

They found a restaurant with outdoor seating nearby and ordered pink lemonade.

As soon as the waitress left, Andi said, "You sure had me scared!"

Troy replied, "Just being near peanuts makes me feel sick."

"What happens if you eat any?"

"I was three when I ate peanuts for the first time and almost died. Then I accidentally had a bite of them in Chinese food a couple of years ago. That also landed me in the hospital."

"What exactly happens to you?"

"My immune system goes berserk. The throat gets swollen, and I have trouble breathing. In other words, I have an attack of anaphylaxis."

"Is there any treatment?"

"I'm supposed to use the auto-injector as soon as I've swallowed or come in contact with peanuts."

"You have to inject yourself with a drug?"

"Yeah, with epinephrine."

Andi thought about this and then asked, "Is it pre-measured, then?"

"Sure."

"Where do you inject it into your body?"

Troy replied, "Any place would be okay, but I usually do it in my belly. It's not supposed to go into muscle."

And he tapped his abdomen, saying, "There's plenty of fat here."

"Did you inject the medication before I came out of the bakery?"

"No. I don't have the auto-injector with me; I left it in my room."

"We'd better rush back, then, so you can have your treatment."

"I'm fine. My throat is feeling better and I'm breathing normally. After all, I didn't eat any; I just inhaled some."

Andi smiled and said, "As for the auto-injector, like the commercial goes, *don't leave home without it!*"

The boy grinned. "You're funny!"

They sat quietly for a while, watching the tourists walk by. Then she said, "I just thought of the nicknames you gave people. Is Mrs. Garcia, 'the general,' some kind of tyrant?"

"I don't know her, but Lupe said she was strict with the maids."

"My favorite is Ms. Dugat as 'the court taster'! Was it your idea to make Mrs. Camden 'the Pope'?"

"Lupe came up with that. I'm Jewish."

When they walked back to where the bike was parked, he confided, "I don't know what Lupe saw or heard, but she must've suspected someone."

"Suspected of the thefts, you mean?"

"Yeah."

"What makes you think that?"

"She was sharp. She was the kind of person who'd ask questions if she suspected anything."

"I see. So you don't think her drowning was an accident?"

Troy shook his head.

Andi glanced at him. His lips were pressed together and there was a stern look in his eyes. She knew that this was all the boy was going to tell.

She gently squeezed his shoulder and said, "We'd better get back in time for dinner or 'the Pope' will miss you and raise hell!"

Chapter 33

A fair amount of people congregated in the recreation hall after dinner that evening. Two of the younger students played a game of ping-pong; others were throwing darts at a target board mounted on the wall. Olivia was trying her best to teach Susie how to shoot pool, without much success. Susie had trouble enough holding the cue, let alone making contact with the billiard ball. She seemed to have a good time nonetheless. Mrs. Brackenbury, Ms. Dugat, Roland Wempel and Paula Parsall were engaged in a bridge game. At one of the small tables for two, Troy was playing chess against Chad Richmond. The man seemed distracted, however. He kept glancing in the direction of another table where Iris Camden and Valencia Kirkland sat. The two ladies were in the middle of a scrabble game, but the actress did more talking than playing.

She said, "Now Iris, you've got to admit that my stay here is less than satisfactory this time."

"I'm sorry, Valencia. What can I do to make you more comfortable?"

"It's not you; I always enjoy your company."

Iris said, "I'm really sorry for what happened with your bracelet."

"I'm not talking about that. There's a gloomy atmosphere here, and it gives me the creeps. I never felt it on my previous visits, but there is definitely something eerie going on now."

"Don't say that, Valencia. I know the pranks that someone pulled are not amusing, but I'm working hard at discovering who's to blame."

"I'm thinking of leaving."

Iris implored, "Please give us another chance. I'll try to make it up to you."

Valencia sighed and continued, "My fellow patrons are no fun either. That boring surgeon is only interested in birds. I tried to have a conversation with him the other day, but he told me to be quiet so he could listen to a woodpecker. Adam Applebee gives me the evil eye whenever our paths cross. Thank goodness that happens seldom, since he tends to stay in his room."

"I'm sorry you feel that way. Most patrons come here for privacy, and I have to respect that."

"Well, I was exhausted after shooting my last movie on location, so I came to relax. It's not working; I'm a nervous wreck."

All of a sudden the actress laughed and remarked, "The only interesting person is the new patron, and he only has eyes for you!"

Iris didn't sound convincing when she replied, "You're imagining things."

Valencia glanced around the room and asked, "Where's Jeffrey hiding this evening?"

"His leg is acting up, so he went to bed early. Let's finish the game and then I'll check up on him. Your turn."

As Iris looked up, she met Chad's admiring eyes. She quickly turned away and thought, he's been following me around all day like a puppy dog and now he seems mesmerized. How ridiculous! He shouldn't have come. I've got to do something about him. Then she focused her mind back on the scrabble game and decided to let Valencia win. At the same time she heard Troy say, "Check mate!"

Chapter 34

As usual, Brant Ronnquist got up early the next morning. He let himself out by the side door at the patron wing. The air was crisp, and he walked briskly on the path along the putting green. He waved to Jeffrey Camden, who was already out practicing his putting skills, and then headed for the woods.

While he hiked on the dirt trail, his mind flashed back to the same scene for the umpteenth time. He was in the operating room at Mount Vargas Hospital. The head nurse said urgently, "Doctor, are you all right?" He had felt dizzy and could not focus; the patient on the operating table in front of him had become nothing but a blur. He had nearly blacked out and managed to say, "Take over, please," to the team of doctors and nurses before he staggered out of the operating theater. Why had he almost fainted? Probably from stress, fatigue, and being overworked. The patient had died of complications unrelated to the surgery. So why did he suffer the reoccurring nightmare? And why couldn't he stop blaming himself? Because as unrealistic as he knew it was, he felt responsible for that patient's death. As top surgeon he was in charge and should not have relied on his subordinates to complete the procedure.

He mused further, coming to this place did help some. He needed the rest, and his hobby of bird-watching truly relaxed him. He wondered if his friend, Eddie the summer tanager, would be waiting for him in the clearing again. Once there, he did his best inviting whistle, interspersed with the typical tanager call of harsh, clicking "pit-i-tuck," to attract his feathered friend. A wood warbler answered his calling, but Eddie was nowhere in sight. He lingered for a while, repeating his beckoning call. Then he looked through his binoculars and searched the area around the clearing, to no avail. He finally focused them farther into the distance and downward below the trees in the hopes of spotting the red bird. What's that huddle on the putting green? he marveled. He adjusted the binoculars to get a clearer image. "Oh, my God!" he yelled out loud, and then ran down the hill.

Getting to the scene, he stopped for a second at the edge of the green. Jeffrey Camden lay in a heap with his head and face in a pool of blood. As he got closer, the doctor realized that the man was beyond help, but he checked for vital signs nonetheless. He was no forensics expert, but he guessed that Mr. Camden had been dead roughly 20 minutes. Then he noticed the putter tossed about a yard away from the body. Obviously, someone had struck Mr. Camden several times with it. Must have happened soon after I saw him, he thought sadly.

Then he walked rapidly toward the building to alert the household.

Chapter 35

On that Thursday in the late afternoon, R.A. Huber was ready to lock up her office and leave for the gym, when Andi called.

Huber asked, "Any more thefts?"

"Mrs. Camden's paperweight is missing, but that ain't important now. There's been a murder!"

"Oh no! Who was killed?"

"Mr. Camden."

Huber sank into her chair and said, "Andi, please calm down, and tell me everything you know about it."

"I came out of the side door ready to go on my early morning walk, when Dr. Ronnquist almost collided with me. He told me that Mr. Camden was bludgeoned to death. Then he asked if I carried a phone, and when I said yes, he ordered me to call 911 and also tell Mrs. Camden. The doctor went back to stay with the body until the police showed up."

"And?"

"First I made the call, and then I went upstairs to get Mrs. Demitris. I had to knock at her door several times before she heard me. She opened the door in her robe; I'd obviously woken her up. After I told her the shocking news, we went to the Camden suite together."

"Why did you alert the school principal first?"

Andi replied, "I did it on impulse. I figured that Mrs. Camden needed somebody besides me to lean on when hearing about her husband. After all, the two women are friends."

"Good judgment, Andi! Please continue."

"Mrs. Camden seemed in shock at first, and then she wanted to rush to the putting green. Mrs. Demitris managed to stop her, and they went to the kitchen, where the cook gave her a drink."

"I assume that the authorities are there now?"

"Yeah, they're here. Most of them are deputy sheriffs. I think they also called in extra help from San Bernardino."

"Did they question you?"

"Not yet. They started with Dr. Ronnquist. Then they talked with Mrs. Camden for a long time, followed by the other patrons. They're questioning Mrs. Demitris now, and I guess the rest of the staff's turn comes next. One at a time, I mean. At this pace, they won't get around to the clients and students until tomorrow."

"You told me that Mr. Camden was bludgeoned to death. Do you know with what weapon?"

"His own putter, it looked like."

"You saw the body?"

"Sure did. After Mrs. Camden was safely in the kitchen, I walked to the green. Dr. Ronnquist seemed to be in charge, so I told him that officers from the Sheriff's Department were on their way and that I'd informed Mrs. Camden."

Huber said, "Which gave you a good excuse to see the murder scene."

"Right, but I had a hard time not puking when I saw Mr. Camden. His face and head was a mess. Someone must've hit him hard many times. His putter that he'd used to practice with lay close by and it was all bloody."

"A brutal crime, no doubt."

Then Andi said, "I can't even grill anyone. Do I blow my cover now?"

Huber replied, "Hold off a little longer, if you can." And she added, "I'll give the police some time, but then I think it's best if I come up to Big Bear."

"I'm sorry, boss. I had no clue and didn't see it coming."

"Neither did I. So don't blame yourself."

Andi's reply of "Okay boss," sounded shaky, and Huber realized that the girl was frightened. So she said, "You couldn't have prevented Mr. Camden's murder, so promise me that you won't torment yourself."

"I won't, ma'am."

On that note, they ended the call.

Chapter 36

At nine o'clock that same evening, Peter answered the phone and then went to the computer room, where Regula sat answering e-mails.

He said, "It's your assistant. She sounds upset."

She grabbed the phone from him. "Hi, Andi. Do you have more bad news?"

"Troy had an attack at dinner and was taken to the hospital."

"What kind of attack?"

"He's allergic to peanuts and must've eaten some."

"Tell me exactly what happened."

"It's a long story. I'm calling from my room. Cyrilla went out, but I'll have to change the subject if she comes back."

"That's understood."

"At dinner tonight, there was a commotion at the clients' table. When I looked over and saw Troy gasping for air, I knew what was happening. So - -"

"Why did you know?"

"He had a reaction yesterday from just smelling the stuff," and Andi related the episode at the bakery.

"Sorry I interrupted, please continue."

"As I said, I knew what was going on. So I rushed over and told Mr. Wempel to call 911. Then I asked Troy where he kept his medication. He couldn't talk, and I shouted, 'In your bathroom?' He shook his head with great effort between labored breathing. 'Where in your bedroom, then?' He was beyond nodding or shaking his head. So I raced to his room and pulled open all the dresser drawers. I finally found the auto-injector in his nightstand.

"When I got back to the dining hall, several people where hovering over Troy, including Mrs. Camden. I pushed everyone out of the way. He was in bad shape by that time. His eyes were closed and his breath came out in short gasps. I was sure glad that he and I had talked about this before so I knew what to do. I stuck the auto-injector into his belly."

Huber said, "Courageous of you, Andi! You probably saved his life."

"Well, remembering how I had to inject my aunt with insulin a few times came in handy."

Andi concluded, "We soon heard sirens, and then the paramedics took over and drove him away in the ambulance. I pray that he pulls through."

Huber could hear the strain in Andi's voice and said, "You like the boy a lot, don't you?"

"Sure do. We were gonna get tutored again tonight. Mrs. Brackenbury cancelled, partly because of Mr. Camden's murder, but mainly because of Troy. We didn't wanna go through with the lesson without him."

"Was there a peanut product in the food?"

"The cook swears that there wasn't. There must've been, though. Before Troy's plate and drink were taken away, Ms. Dugat dumped everything into plastic bags for analysis."

"Good for her!" Huber said. Then she asked, "Do you know who's aware of Troy's allergy?"

Andi replied, "Ms. Dugat, of course. She must've put the information on Troy's chart. I bet the cook was told, so he'd avoid putting peanut products in meals. I'd guess that Troy's parents told Mrs. Camden when they enrolled him. It's possible that some clients and students also know about it."

"What is Troy's last name and where do his parents live?"

"Their name is Hesselman and they live in San Diego."

"Do you know to which hospital he was driven?"

Andi answered, "I think to the one in Big Bear." Then she abruptly changed her tone of voice and said, "Wonderful! Nice talking with you, Auntie Betsy, and say hello to Uncle Buba!"

Huber said, "So your roommate has returned! Take care of yourself. I'll see you soon." Then she hung up.

Chapter 37

When Regula joined him in the living room, Peter asked, "Another murder?"

"Attempted, this time. I hope the victim is still alive." Then she recounted her conversation with Andi.

He asked, "What are you going to do?"

"It's too late in the evening now, but tomorrow I'll try to contact Troy's parents."

"To find out how the boy is doing?"

"That, plus warn them."

"Meaning?"

"If he's still in the hospital by tomorrow, I'll suggest that they transfer him somewhere else, without telling anyone the new location."

"So you suspect the villain will try to finish the job, if Troy is alive?"

She nodded.

"You think that the boy knows something?"

"I have no idea, but the murderer evidently is of that opinion."

After a pause Peter said, "Do you believe that the earlier thefts and pranks are somehow linked to Jeffrey Camden's murder?"

"They must be. Coincidences like that just don't happen."

"How do you think they are connected?"

"If I knew that, I could tell you who the murderer is."

"What about the maid's drowning?"

"She must have known or suspected who the culprit was and questioned the person. At first I thought that killing for the sake of the transgressions was farfetched. Now, with a second murder and an attempted murder, my attitude has changed."

"What are you going to do other than warning Troy's folks?"

"It's time for me to pay Optimum House a visit."

Peter remarked, "I had a hunch that was your plan!"

Chapter 38

On Friday evening, Cyrilla and Andi faced Mrs. Demitris in her office. Glancing at the modeling school principal, Andi thought that Troy's nickname for the lady, the prototype, was appropriate. Her posture and everything about her was perfect. She looked like the prototype of a model.

She said to the two young women, "I decided to talk with you both together. Normally, Mrs. Camden handles these things. Under the circumstances, I don't want to bother her. She's struggling with making funeral arrangements and dealing with the authorities."

Cyrilla thought, shit! I'm found out! She's going to expel me. Andi was thinking, shit! I somehow blew my cover.

Mrs. Demitris continued, "After looking at your photos, an agent of Fielding, the number one modeling agency in New York is interested in both of you. He wants to see you in person."

The young women stared.

Then Cyrilla said, "The pictures went out already?"

"It's all done electronically. The photographer sent them to several agencies via e-mail. As I said, we got a response from Fielding, New York."

As the good news registered with Cyrilla, she shouted, "Hallelujah!" Then she asked, "Who else are we in competition with?"

"The agent is only interested in you two."

Cyrilla nudged Andi and said, "Girl! We're going to New York!"

Andi tried her best to look enthusiastic, but didn't quite succeed.

Mrs. Demitris said, "You don't seem excited, Andi."

"Guess I'm in shock. Didn't expect it."

"Isn't your purpose in attending this school to be noticed by a top agency?"

Andi stuttered, "It's only natural that they'd want Cyrilla; she's perfect. But me? You said yourself, ma'am, that I needed lots of work."

"That's true, but your shortcomings don't show up in photos. Anyhow, our spring session ends July 3. Then there's the Fourth of July holiday weekend, so I scheduled you both for an interview July 6. You can fly to New York on the fifth and spend the night. Either Mrs. Camden or I will accompany you."

When the young people got to their room, Cyrilla flopped down on her bed, buried her face in her palms, and sobbed.

"What's the matter?" Andi asked.

Cyrilla pulled herself together and said, "With all the horrible stuff that's happened here, I thought that coming to this school was a mistake. And now I have the chance of a lifetime: an interview with Fielding, the hottest agency in New York, and I can't go!"

"Why not?"

"I'm having my surgery July 6."

"Can't you postpone it?"

"Don't you see? I need the operation before I become a model."

"Then reschedule the interview."

"That's not how it works. The big guys call the shots. You go when they wanna see you, or you've missed the boat."

Andi said, "July 6 is over a month away. We'll figure out something."

Chapter 39

R. A. Huber arrived at Optimum House on the following Monday morning. Iris was on the phone when the private investigator opened the door to the administrative office. She motioned the visitor in and pointed to the chair in front of her desk. Regula sat down, startled by the change in Iris. It was hard to believe that this was the elegant, self-assured and confident person who came to consult her less than three weeks ago. The woman she saw now looked years older, miserable and defeated. Then her eyes came to rest on the castle paperweight sitting on the desk.

Iris continued her phone conversation, "I understand - - I'm sorry - - yes, of course - -we'll expect you tomorrow, then - - thank you."

She hung up and said, "Well, Mrs. Huber, this was the third parent that called to let me know she's taking her student out of the school. I'm sure there will be more before the day is over."

"I'm sorry."

"The person who's out to ruin me succeeded. Now, with Jeffrey gone, I hardly care any longer."

Huber focused on the castle again and remarked, "What an unusual paperweight!"

A melancholy smile spread over Iris's face as she said, "Jeffrey gave it to me when we first opened the school, saying 'Here's a castle for my queen!'"

"Is this the paperweight that disappeared?"

"How did you know it was taken?"

"Andi periodically called to keep me informed."

"Of course. How stupid of me."

"When did you first miss it, and when and where did it turn up again?"

"I noticed that it was gone when I came into my office Wednesday morning. Someone put it back on my desk on Thursday. By that time I'd learned about Jeffrey, and the paperweight was unimportant."

Huber said, "I understand. Still, I'd like to know when exactly on Thursday you noticed that the castle was returned."

Iris sighed and replied, "I was barely aware of it, but when the sheriff questioned me it was back on the desk."

"I hate to add to your burden, but I need to ask more questions."

"The police have taken over."

"I'm aware of that, but I'd like to stay on the case if that's all right with you."

"Of course you may! The sooner we catch the criminal, the better." Then she asked, "You're planning to stay with us?"

"If it's not too much trouble."

"No problem. We've got plenty of room." And with a frown she added, "Soon we'll have so much extra room we won't know what to do with it."

Looking at the grief-stricken woman, Huber said, "Do you feel up to giving me information now, or shall I come back later?"

"Let's get it over with right away."

"First, tell me a little about your staff. How long has each person been employed?"

"All right. Dolores Garcia, the head housekeeper, has been with us since we started nine years ago. At first she managed with only two maids. When we got bigger and added programs, she needed more help. Currently, Mrs. Garcia has six - - I mean five - - domestics under her wing. Emma Demitris asked me for a position in the modeling school soon after her divorce, and I was more than happy to take her on board. That was seven years ago. I found a jewel when I hired the cook, Isandro Jimenez. Amazing the tasty meals he creates, given the low-calorie diets he needs to adhere to. He's been here five years, first alone and now with two assistants. It's been about four years since Kathleen Brackenbury joined us. She's much more competent than the prior tutor we had. Nadine Dugat replaced the former dietitian who retired two years ago. I also hired our male student instructor, Ralph Smith, at around the same time. He's not a live-in and resides in Big Bear City.

"That's it, I think. I don't know offhand how long each of the domestic helpers has been employed, but I can look up their records."

Huber said, "Thanks, but that isn't necessary. I also don't think that your outside help, like the beauticians or photographer, for instance, are involved. The thefts and pranks had to be done by someone living on the premises. The same applies to your husband's killer since it happened early in the morning."

At the mention of Jeffrey's murder, Iris flinched. But then she managed to nod her head.

The private eye continued, "Tell me about the maid that drowned. I think Lupe is her name."

"Oh, but that was an accident; the sheriff was sure of that."

"The way things stand now, we have to look at the drowning from a different perspective."

"You think her accident is connected to Jeffrey's murder?"

"Logically, yes."

Iris said, "This was only Lupe's first season with us. I didn't know her well. I'm sure Mrs. Garcia can tell you more about her."

"Who hired her?"

"I do all job interviewing and hiring." And she added, "Like I already told you, I had no idea the young woman couldn't swim."

"Yes, I remember. Have you filled her position yet?"

"No, and it looks like there is no need for a replacement now."

Then Regula asked, "Do all of the domestics understand and speak English?"

"Some don't, but I'm fluent in Spanish."

"I see."

Neither woman spoke for some time. Regula looked out the window onto the parking lot. Glancing at the Harley-Davidson, she thought, hope I'll find an opportunity to talk with Andi soon. Then she felt it was time to get to the nitty-gritty.

She said, "I know this won't be easy for you, Mrs. Camden, but tell me your account of what happened early Thursday morning."

"I understand." She appeared to be in control, and her voice was steady when she began, "Your assistant and Emma woke me up and told me that Dr. Ronnquist had found Jeffrey dead. I wasn't fully awake and thought I was having a bad dream. When the news sank in, I didn't want to believe it. Then I threw on a dressing gown and was on my way to the putting green, but Emma stopped me. She took me to the kitchen instead, where she told Mr. Jimenez that I'd had a shock, and he gave me some brandy."

"At what time was that?"

"It must've been around seven because the kitchen crew was rolling trays of breakfast food into the dining hall."

"Did you go to the murder scene later?"

Iris was holding back tears as she answered, "By the time Emma and I came out of the kitchen, the authorities had arrived. I wanted to go and see Jeffrey, but the officer wouldn't let me."

"Do you know what time it was when Mr. Camden left your suite that morning?"

"I was asleep and didn't hear him go out."

"What can you tell me about Troy Hesselman's attack?"

Iris replied, "I feel awful about what happened to the boy." She then related what she'd witnessed at dinner that evening. Her story tallied with what Huber had already learned from Andi.

"Did you know that Troy was allergic to peanuts?"

"Of course."

"Who else knew?"

"Everyone at Optimum House."

"Everyone?"

"The allergy was the first thing his parents mentioned when they enrolled him. So I alerted the cook and Ms. Dugat right away. Troy was so highly allergic that it was prudent to make everyone aware of the fact. So I announced it at dinner when all were present."

"Andi told me that the dietitian collected samples from Troy's food and drink for analysis. Are the results already known?"

Iris stated, "There was crude peanut oil in the salad dressing. Mr. Jimenez makes his own dressing and swears that he never used peanut oil. He insists that there are no peanut products kept in his kitchen." She sighed and continued, "I believe him. He's been our cook for five years and is extremely conscientious."

"Yes, I see."

"By the way, I called the hospital the following day to inquire about Troy. They said that the boy was transferred

somewhere else and refused to tell me where. Can you
believe it?"

Huber answered, "It never hurts to be cautious."

"What do you mean?"

"I think you know."

At that moment Emma Demitris opened the door and
peeked in. She addressed Iris, saying, "Sorry to interrupt,
but reporters from a couple of newspapers are here."

"Tell them 'no comment,'" Iris ordered.

"I think it would be wise to make some kind of a
statement."

Iris thought it over and then said, "You may be right.
I don't have the stomach to talk to them, so please handle
it for me, Emma."

"No problem," the principal said, and retreated.

Then Huber asked, "Are the authorities still on the
premises?"

"Not at the moment, but they'll be back as soon as all
the parents have arrived."

"I don't understand."

"They've questioned everyone except the students
who are minors. At least one parent needs to be present
during their interviews."

"Yes, of course." And after a pause she continued, "Do
the police know that you hired me, and are they aware of
Andi's position?"

Iris replied, "Yes. Under the circumstances, I felt
obliged to tell them. I also let Emma know this morning
and informed her that I expected you today. At this point
I'm sure it makes no difference about being discreet; the
reputation and good standing of my business is already
ruined."

"I'd like to talk with Mr. Jimenez and Mrs. Garcia first.
Can that be arranged?"

"Emma will see to it. She has been a tremendous help and support to me these last few days. I couldn't cope without her."

"One more thing. Are the students' classes and the schedules for the health-program clients cancelled?"

"No. I thought it best to keep things running as routinely as possible. When the police question each person in turn, the students are excused from class, the health-program clients interrupt their programs and the staff halt their work."

Huber inquired, "When would be a good time and place to have everyone, except the domestic staff, assemble in a large room? I need to make a statement."

"You mean everybody together?"

"Yes, please."

Iris took a moment before she said, "Everyone comes to the dining hall for dinner at the same time."

"Good. I'll make my announcement right after dinner."

Chapter 40

Isandro Jimenez muttered to himself, first the police accused me of having peanut oil in my kitchen and now some woman investigator wants to grind me. The small man shook his curly black hair, now streaked with gray. His dark-brown eyes expressed indignation as he walked toward the east wing. Before this day, he'd never had occasion to visit any of the patrons. In the five years he had worked here, he'd only ventured from the domestics' residence to the ground floor of the main building, mostly to the kitchen and back. Occasionally, he was asked to see Ms. Dugat in her office, and if Mrs. Camden made a special menu request for any of the patrons, he would go to the administrative office.

The latest situation at Optimum House was unsettling for Isandro. He had quit his job as chef at a first-rate gourmet restaurant because at the age of 60 the demands on him became too stressful. The position here had suited him perfectly. The workplace was pleasant, and he shared a small apartment in the domestics' quarters with Margarita, his wife. Now, all hell had broken loose, he thought. First there had been the silly thefts, then Mr. Camden's murder, and on the very same evening, the incident with the kid.

With each step he took, his facial expression became grimmer. Maybe it was time for him to retire, he concluded. After all, he'd turned 65 and had a little nest egg put aside. With it, Margarita and he could live a good life in Costa Rica, the country of his ancestors. If it weren't for poor Mrs. Camden, he'd quit his job right away. As it was, he couldn't bring himself to abandon her at the time of her grief. She had been the most wonderful boss anyone could ask for. The lady was a beauty, no doubt, but that wasn't all. He didn't know why, but he always felt happy when in her presence. He wished there was something he could do to ease her burden. At this point in his train of thought, he stood at the door of Huber's suite and knocked.

Chapter 41

While Regula unpacked and stowed away her belongings in the spacious suite, she mulled over the conversation she had just had with Mrs. Camden. Astounding how, although overwhelmed with sorrow, the woman was able to make rational decisions. She had insisted on a patron suite, pointing out that its size and comfort would be useful when questioning suspects. Regula smiled to herself, knowing that any room with two chairs would have done. Then she looked at her watch and thought, 10:30; Andi must be in class. I wonder if she carries her phone. I'll call her at noon.

Suddenly she heard knocking at the door and went to open it.

The man standing in the doorway said, "I'm Isandro Jimenez. You wanted to see me?" Though he was clearly Latino, Regula detected no accent in his speech.

She replied, "Yes, please come in, Mr. Jimenez," and led him to the comfortable sofa.

Before she could begin with the interview he said, "I know nothing about Mr. Camden's murder, and there was no peanut oil in the health clients' salad dressing, at least not when I prepared it."

"I'm sure that's true, but I'd like to ask you a few questions anyway. I'm R.A. Huber, by the way."

"Go ahead, Mrs. Huber."

"First, let's talk about the misdeeds that occurred in the last month."

"That was just petty thefts and silly pranks. Childish, if you ask me."

Huber said, "Stealing a diamond bracelet is not petty theft in my book."

"I forgot about the bracelet," he replied.

"I understand that you found Dr. Ronnquist's missing binoculars. Is that correct?"

"That's right. I remember that he made a big fuss when they were lifted from him. He was standing in the hallway and shouted, 'What impertinence! Someone stole my binoculars!' He yelled this so loud that I could hear him from my kitchen. A couple of days later, when I started work in the morning, they showed up in one of my cupboards among the spices."

"You don't lock the kitchen at night?"

"No, never have."

Then Huber said, "Please tell me about Thursday morning."

"From the time I got up?"

"Let's say, starting with when you walked from your residence to the main building."

"At 6:45 a.m. I went straight to the kitchen, as usual. My assistants were already there, had brewed coffee, squeezed orange juice, and were getting organized with the continental breakfast. I gave them a hand, and then they rolled or carried things into the dining hall. I checked the in-basket for any orders from the patrons. There was only one from Mr. Applebee. He wanted - -"

"Before you go on, please explain the continental breakfast to me."

"What do you mean?"

"I'd like to know what is served."

"We don't serve breakfast. We just lay food out at the end of the tables and people help themselves. There's a slight difference between the breakfasts for the health-program clients and the students. We keep each at separate tables. The dairy products, for instance, are nonfat for clients and low-fat for students. The staff can help themselves from either and so can the patrons, or they may give a special order. Typically, our breakfast consists of a variety of fresh fruit, bread, whole-wheat English muffins, margarine, preserves, cereal and yogurt. For beverages there is coffee, tea, milk, freshly squeezed orange juice and water."

"Sorry I interrupted. You were saying that there was an order from Mr. Applebee in the in-basket."

Isandro continued, "He wanted waffles topped with strawberries and whipped cream. So I started to fix that."

"I'm not sure I understand the concept of your in-basket. I mean, how are the orders placed?"

"Did you notice the small box next to your door?"

"I thought it was a mailbox, assuming that patrons on a prolonged stay might have their mail forwarded."

"No, that is where they can place their breakfast orders the night before, if they want it brought to their room. A maid checks the boxes first thing in the morning and brings the orders - if there are any - to the kitchen, where she puts them in the in-basket."

"I see."

"If the patrons who eat their breakfast in the dining hall request any special food, they can give me the order directly, and I'll turn into a short-order cook," he said with a grin.

Huber stated, "All right, I'm clear on that. Getting back to Thursday morning, what happened next?"

"I'd just poured the batter into the waffle iron, when Mrs. Demitris led Mrs. Camden into the kitchen. Even if both women hadn't been in their robes, I'd have known right away that something was wrong when I glanced at my employer. She looked like a ghost. Then the principal told me that Mrs. Camden had had a great shock and was there anything I could give her. I brought her a stool to sit on and then rushed to the liquor cabinet and poured her some brandy. Then I asked what the trouble was and Mrs. Demitris told me." He added, "Suddenly, I smelled something burning and realized I had forgotten about the waffle in the iron and ruined it."

After a pause Huber asked, "Did you see anyone either outside or in the house when you walked to the kitchen to start your day?"

He took some time to think and then said, "I saw a maid going into the pool area, probably to clean it. And of course my two helpers were in the kitchen when I got there."

"Anyone else? I'm thinking of the patrons, students and clients."

He shook his head.

"Speaking of maids, did you know the young woman who drowned in the pool?"

"Lupe and I said hi when we ran into one another, but I hardly knew her."

"Your two assistants, do they speak English?"

"Not much."

"So you speak Spanish, then?"

"I was born in the U.S. but brought up bilingual. My parents emigrated from Costa Rica."

She continued, "I understand that a student's motorcycle goggles were sitting on top of Adam Applebee's breakfast the other day."

"Yes, I heard. Mr. Applebee was mad and made a fuss, and who could blame him?"

"Was it you or one of your assistants that cooked the breakfast?"

"I fixed Applebee's breakfast myself, as my two helpers were busy with putting the continental breakfast together."

"Any idea how the goggles got on the plate?"

"They were certainly not put there by me or my men. There was only bacon, scrambled eggs and toast on that dish when it left the kitchen."

"Who brought it to Mr. Applebee's suite?"

"A maid."

"What's her name?"

"I don't know."

Surprised, Huber said, "You didn't see her?"

"No. I placed the breakfast tray on the alcove between the kitchen and hallway, and the maid took it from there. I believe her code was 34."

"I don't understand."

"The maids rotate their jobs. Whoever had east wing duty that week took the breakfast and carried it to Mr. Applebee's suite."

"I still don't follow you. What kind of code do you mean?"

"It's simple. Every maid carries a buzzer. The little gadget is not as sophisticated as a cell phone; it's more like a pager. We enter the code number and the maid gets a buzz. The location or person where the beep comes from is displayed on her device, also with a code." With a spark of humor he continued, "So she drops everything and rushes to where the buzzer tells her to go."

"I'm beginning to understand now. Wait a minute. If you don't know which maid is on that particular duty, how do you figure out what code to enter?"

Isandro said, "Now I see why you're a detective! It's not at all high tech! The same maid is collecting the breakfast orders first thing in the morning and puts them in the in-basket with her code number written on the orders."

Huber agreed, "As you said, quite simple!" Then she said, "We need to talk about what happened to Troy Hesselman."

Isandro had started to warm up to the lady sleuth, but at the mention of the boy's name he stiffened and his facial expression turned hostile.

He replied, "The police implied that there was peanut oil in my salad dressing, but I set them straight. I don't cook with peanut oil, nor do I put any in my dressing. There is no such oil in my entire kitchen."

"You knew that Troy was allergic to peanuts?"

"Of course. That was the reason I didn't keep any peanut products around."

"Do you make your own dressing?"

"Yes, I do."

"Do you mind telling me what goes in it?"

He stated, "For the health-program clients I make vinaigrette using rice vinegar and sesame oil and add just a pinch of garlic salt to give it extra flavor. This salad dressing is low in fat and healthy. The students get a choice of the vinaigrette or a low-fat Italian dressing. The patrons may have anything from French, Thousand Island, zesty Italian, blue cheese, Roquefort to honey-mustard."

"Do you prepare them all from scratch or do you also use store brands?"

"I make them all myself, and none of them have peanut oil in them."

Then she asked, "Do you mix the dressings ahead of time?"

"Yes, the basic ones: vinaigrette, low-fat Italian, French and zesty Italian. The rest on patrons' demand."

"And I presume none can be mistaken for any of the others?"

"Of course not," he replied, seemingly offended. "I keep them in separate containers and label them clearly."

Huber stated, "I think we covered everything. I don't want to keep you away from your kitchen any longer this close to lunchtime. Thank you for coming. Oh, and please ask your helpers if they saw anyone on their way to the kitchen before starting work on Thursday morning."

As he got up to leave, she asked, "Do you like your job as cook at this establishment, Mr. Jimenez?"

"Until a few days ago I was happy here. Now I'm depressed."

Chapter 42

Dolores Garcia was not happy as she walked rapidly toward the east wing. She thought, a woman private investigator wants to interrogate me! How did she suddenly appear out of nowhere? And lodging in one of the patron's suites, no less! Guess I can't refuse to talk to her since Mrs. Camden wants me to.

At 5'6" she was considered tall for someone of Mexican heritage. Although in her mid-fifties, her dark hair pulled severely away from her face and tied into a chignon showed little gray. Instead of her usual print tops and trousers, today she wore a black skirt and crisp white blouse out of respect for the bereaved.

She dwelled further on the matter: Bad enough when things kept disappearing and she could tell Mrs. Camden was plenty worried about that. But *murder* at Optimum House! Impossible. The thing was, it *did* happen and Mr. Camden *was* dead. For a moment her expression changed from indignation to sadness as she remembered her former boss. He was a nice man, and nice people didn't get themselves killed. She hated funerals, but she'd have to go to his. That was unavoidable. And the poor Missus was trying to do business as usual, yet it was plain to see that she was suffering terribly.

Then Dolores's thoughts turned personal. She liked her job and she, together with Emilio, had spent nine happy years here. Now there was a crazy killer among them and she was suddenly scared. Her maids were feeling the dread and tension too. She had never seen them this jumpy and irritable before. How and when will it all end? she wondered.

Chapter 43

Moments later Dolores was sitting bolt upright on the edge of the sofa in the patron's suite facing R.A. Huber. The investigator was not at all what she had expected. Her picture of a female private eye had been a tough, powerful person in her prime. This lady was slender, wearing a fashionable fitted dress and heels, and, most surprisingly, was probably older than she.

Regula had introduced herself and asked the housekeeper if she'd like a soda or a drink of water, trying to put her at ease. Dolores had declined and seemed to sit up even straighter, if that was possible. So the former began the interview.

"I understand that you've worked here as housekeeper since the start of the modeling school."

"That's right."

"How did you hear of this job and apply for it?"

"I didn't have to apply; Mrs. Camden got in touch with me."

"Oh, you two knew one another beforehand?"

"Not really. I was the housekeeper for a family in L.A. who were friends with Mrs. Camden's parents. Just before the opening of the school, my employers retired and planned to move away. Mrs. Camden asked me if I'd be interested in a housekeeping position at a boarding school in the Big Bear area. I talked it over with Emilio, my husband. He works in construction, and our kids were grown, so we gave it a try. Emilio found a job in Big Bear City, and we loved our apartment here in the domestics' quarters. So it all worked out."

Huber detected just a trace of an accent in Dolores's speech, but her English was good. So she said, "You must have come to the U.S. at a young age. Your command of the English language is excellent."

Dolores smiled and replied, "Thank you! I was barely 20 when I came to this country."

Now that some of the stiffness had lifted from the housekeeper, Huber felt it was time to get on with the questions and said, "Mrs. Garcia, what can you tell me about the events of Thursday morning?"

"Not much. Thursday is my day off, so I'd planned to drive down to San Bernardino to visit my daughter and see the grandkids. Well, things turned out differently. On my days off I'm usually not in a hurry to get going, so I drink my coffee while reading the paper before I take a shower. When I heard sirens and looked out the window and saw police cars in the parking lot, I threw on a robe over my pajamas and rushed outdoors.

"The new modeling student came running along the outside of the east wing and directed the officers toward the putting green. I knew something awful must have happened, because the student looked as white as a ghost. I was going to follow the officers, but one of them turned around and asked me who I was. 'The housekeeper,' I said, and asked what was going on. He didn't tell me, but ordered the girl and me to go into the main building and keep everyone away from the scene. When we walked inside, the student told me the terrible news about Mr. Camden. Then she stationed herself at the east wing door and I took the main entrance, letting nobody go outside and toward the putting green until a couple of deputy sheriffs took our places."

"Whom did you have to stop?"

"Everyone! People had heard the sirens and gathered in the hallway trying to find out what was going on. I told my maids to go back to their jobs. Students and clients stood around in panic, it seemed. Mrs. Brackenbury kept her cool and told the students to either go into the dining hall for breakfast or else back to their rooms. Ms. Dugat tried to take charge of the health-program people but didn't have much luck in controlling them. Especially one person - - I think her name starts with a 'P' - - who said she wasn't leaving until she got information."

Huber asked, "Paula Parsall?"

"That's the one."

She continued, "Then I saw Mrs. Camden and Mrs. Demitris walking out of the kitchen. Mrs. Camden looked awful, so I'm sure she already knew about the murder. Thank God the law officers took over by that time. I wouldn't have liked to tell Mrs. Camden what she can and can't do."

Dolores sighed and then said, "That's all. Needless to say, I never made it to San Bernardino, since I had to stick around in case the police wanted to question me."

"Did they?"

"Not until the next day, and I told them exactly what I just said to you." And she added, "I can't imagine who murdered Mr. Camden or why."

Dolores had uttered the last words with finality in her voice. There was no point in going on about Thursday's killing, so Regula said, "Let's get to the maid's drowning."

The housekeeper became grave and replied, "So you've heard about Lupe." And after a pause she said, "I'm to blame for her death."

"Oh?"

"She pleaded with me not to assign her to pool duty. She said that she couldn't swim and that she was afraid to go near water. She especially was worried about falling off the diving board while cleaning it. I should've granted her the wish; she did fall off the board and drowned. Of course I didn't let her have her way and made it clear that I expected the domestics to take turns in their respective jobs. As far as being afraid of drowning, I told her 'Nonsense. You've got to overcome your fear by facing it head on.'"

She took a deep breath before she continued, "Lupe was not afraid of me or anyone else and said she'd go directly to Mrs. Camden and ask to be excused from pool duty. Whether or not she actually did go and see her, I don't know. If so, Mrs. Camden must not have given in to her either."

"What kind of person was Lupe?"

"She was only 18, intelligent, and planned to go to college the next year. She was also a good and fast worker."

"Was she close to any of the other maids?"

"I don't think so. She kept to herself, and on her days off I often saw her in the library with her head in a book instead of going out. She was a lot younger than the other maids and didn't have much in common with them. She befriended one of the clients, a young boy. I tried to discourage the friendship; I don't think it's a good idea for domestics to mix with clients or students socially. Well, I told you that Lupe wasn't afraid of me. She said that what she did on her time off was none of my business."

Dolores vocalized that last sentence with a sad smile, and Regula, sensing that there was more Mrs. Garcia needed to get off her chest, waited.

After a few moments silence the housekeeper said in rapid speech, "Why must I be such a tyrant? Why couldn't I just for once let Lupe have her way? What harm could have been done if another maid had taken pool duty instead? Why do I insist on always having control over my charges? If it weren't for my stupid pride, the girl would still be alive."

Then she calmed down and said, "Sorry for the outburst, but I ask myself these questions every single day since Lupe drowned."

Huber said, "But I'm the first person you shared this with?"

Dolores nodded.

"It helps to let it out, doesn't it?" Then she changed the subject and said, "Did you witness Troy Hesselman's attack on Thursday evening?"

"No, but I learned about it later. The boy got sick in the dining hall. I never eat there and neither do my maids. We fix our meals in our own apartments. I was cooking dinner for Emilio and me when we heard sirens again. This time it was the paramedics."

"You knew that Troy was allergic to peanuts, though?"

"Oh yes. Everyone knew."

Then Regula said, "I heard that you discovered one of the stolen items in a flower bouquet in the dining hall."

"Yes, I was adding water to the vase when I found the teacher's grading sheet stuck between the leaves. Since it was shortly before lunch, I waited for Mrs. Brackenbury and handed it to her when she came in. She didn't seem upset about its disappearance and just said, 'Oh, you found my grading list. Thank you.'"

"Do you know which maid carried the breakfast with the goggles to Mr. Applebee?"

"Rosalia was on duty at the patrons' wing that week, but I'm sure she had nothing to do with the prank."

"I don't think so either, but may I briefly talk with Rosalia if you can spare her for a few minutes this afternoon?"

"I'll send her over."

"Oh, and do you remember which maid found the student's dress cut to pieces?"

Dolores's expression turned solemn as she said, "It was Lupe. She came to me carrying the laundry room wastebasket and showed me the shreds."

Then Regula asked, "What do you make of these thefts and mischief that have occurred since the beginning of the spring session?"

"At first I thought it was all silly doings by spirited students. Now I wonder if we have a crazy criminal in the household who started with taking and destroying things and then went berserk and is murdering people now."

"Interesting thought," Huber commented.

Chapter 44

When Andi showed up at the suite, she was clad in a stylish shift and was wearing her new pumps. Her thick auburn hair, held back neatly with barrettes matching the chartreuse color of her dress, cascaded down her back in controlled waves. Gone were the leather jacket, jeans and boots.

"Well, Andi, you look lovely! They've tamed you!" Huber remarked.

"Only on the outside," she replied with a grin.

Then she looked around at the spacious accommodations. She glanced from the sofa group to the bookshelf, then to the vase of yellow roses sitting on the table, the fabulous DVD system and the big screen TV. There was an upright piano standing against one wall.

Andi pointed to it, asking, "You play?"

"No, do you?"

"The fiddle's all I know." Then she said, "So what's it here for?"

"I asked Mrs. Camden the same thing when she showed me in. Evidently, a patron who is a composer had this suite last season and requested a piano."

Andi rolled her eyes and remarked, "So he snapped his fingers and it was delivered!"

Then she walked the length of the room and, looking through the glass door, noticed the massive balcony with a view to the lake.

"Wow! So that's what a patron suite looks like!"

"Wait 'til you see the kitchen, bedroom and bath," Regula commented.

"I think this here is all I can handle for now, thank you, ma'am."

"Let's get down to business, then. On the balcony would be most enjoyable, but we can't take the chance of being overheard. Now that I'm a non-smoker, I don't mind staying inside."

"When did you quit?"

"Three months ago. I've tried to stop a few times before, but now I'm serious about it." Huber rolled up her sleeve and pointed to her upper arm, saying, "See!"

Andi asked "That's a nicotine patch? It's transparent!"

"What did you think they looked like?"

"Oh, I don't know, uglier, for sure."

Huber laughed and said, "So where do you want to sit: on the upholstered chair or sofa?"

"At the table, please, so we can face each other better."

Once established, Huber said, "First off, I'm pleased to tell you that Troy is fine and already went home."

"Oh, I'm so happy he's okay; I was worried sick. Did you talk to him?"

"I spoke with his mother. She said to tell you that you saved her son's life, and as soon as this case is solved, she wants to meet you and thank you in person. Troy can't wait to see you too."

"He's not coming back to Optimum House, is he?"

"No. Under the circumstances we cannot take that chance. Except for you and I, no one knows where he is."

Then she said, "Now let's compare notes. Have you anything new to report since our last phone conversation?"

"Not much. Because of Mr. Camden's murder, people are scared and look at everyone with suspicion. It's business as usual, but there is a glum mood around this place. Everybody is jumpy and watching their backs. Maybe I just imagined it, but Mrs. Demitris looked at me strangely a couple of times in class today. You reckon she thinks I'm the criminal?"

Huber replied, "She knows now that you're my assistant."

"Oh, that must be it!"

"Have you been questioned by the police yet?"

"Sure did, by deputy sheriffs. They knew about me. Mrs. Camden must've told them."

"Did they let you in on anything?"

"I tried to pump them for info, but no luck there."

"Did you tell them anything useful?"

"They knew about the thefts and stuff, but wanted to hear it from me. So I gave them my two cents' worth."

"Which was?"

"I sorta told them who I think didn't do it, but I'm sure they would've figured that out themselves."

Huber said, "Who did you cross off your suspect list?"

"The servants -- I mean the domestic staff -- the male students and their teacher, and the 12 high school kids."

"I agree, but I still would like to hear your reasons."

"Okay boss, this is how I look at it: The domestic help wouldn't dare to do the pranks and stuff, and I can't come up with a motive for them to kill Mr. Camden. They also don't live in the building. The male students and Mr. Smith don't live here at all. Our murderer must be a live-in; some of the monkey business was done at night, I reckon. The 12 girls are wimps. I can't see any of them tackling Mr. Camden. He was a powerful man, banged up knee and all."

Regula said, "You certainly can use your head! I'm pleased with you, Andi."

"Thank you, boss! I'm tickled to death you think so!" And after a pause she asked, "What's your order now?"

"Do you mind going back to class this afternoon and playing the modeling student for just a little longer, until after dinner, to be exact?"

"Sure thing, Mrs. Huber. What happens after dinner?"

"As far as I know, only Mrs. Camden and Mrs. Demitris know about our investigation. So this evening, when everyone will be assembled in the dining hall, I'll spring the news. Then we'll watch their faces and note their reactions."

Andi stated, "I can tell you one thing. The older students are gonna be mad as hell at me."

Huber said, "I imagine so." Then she continued, "I interviewed the cook and head housekeeper this morning. I'll probably talk to Mrs. Demitris in the afternoon, as she already knows who I am. Later, after you're established as assistant sleuth, you can sit in on the questioning. I'll tell you what I learned from Mr. Jimenez and Mrs. Garcia some other time. Right now I'm famished. Let's go to lunch."

Chapter 45

Rosalia was 43, short and on the heavy side. She wore her dark hair shoulder length and usually had a lovely smile and a sparkle in her brown eyes. However, there was no humor in those eyes as she faced the lady detective.

She looked like a scared rabbit as she said in broken English, "I not know anything."

"About the murder, you mean?"

She nodded.

"I'm sure you don't. My questions are about your job. I understand that you brought Mr. Applebee his plate on the morning that he found goggles in his breakfast, correct?"

"I not put goggles there."

"Of course not. Just tell me about your chores when you started work that morning, please."

So she explained how at 6:30 she had first gone from box to box in the patrons' wing to collect breakfast orders. There had only been one that day, and it was from Adam Applebee for bacon, eggs and toast. She had then brought it to the kitchen, wrote her code number on the order sheet, and then placed it into the in-basket. Later, when her buzzer went off, she had walked back and taken the breakfast tray from the alcove and carried it to Mr. Applebee's suite. The gentleman was in the bathroom when she got there and called out to her to leave the tray on the table. She had done so and then left.

Huber asked, "How many minutes passed from the time you placed the order into the basket until you heard the beeper?"

Rosalia shrugged her shoulders and said, "I not know. 20 or 30 minutes?"

"What were you doing when the buzzer rang?"

"I clean and put fresh towels to other gentleman's bath."

"Do you remember the gentleman's name?"

She shook her head and said, "He is doctor."

"Dr. Ronnquist?"

"Yes."

"So you went to clean Dr. Ronnquist's bathroom after you brought the breakfast order to the kitchen, right?"

"Yes, I see he leave and he have - - how do you say?" - - she made circles around her eyes with her thumbs and pointer fingers - - "and go watch the bird."

"Okay, I understand. You saw Dr. Ronnquist leave, carrying his binoculars for bird-watching, and so decided to clean his bathroom."

"Yes."

"Is Dr. Ronnquist's suite on the ground floor or on the second, like mine?"

"Downstairs."

"So when you heard your buzzer go off, you were cleaning his bathroom. How long did it take you to get from his suite back to the kitchen to pick up Mr. Applebee's breakfast?"

She shrugged her shoulders again and said, "First I wash hands. Then I go."

"This is important, Rosalia. Can you estimate how many minutes?"

"Four – five – six, maybe."

"Did you see anyone on your way there?"

"I see Mr. Camden go out."

Probably on his way to the putting green, Regula thought. Then she asked, "Whom else did you see?"

"I see student go dining hall."

"You probably don't know any of their names, but what did the student look like?"

"She tall, big steps, red hair, pretty."

Sounds like Andi, Huber thought.

"Did you see anyone else?"

Rosalia shook her head.

"Too early for most people to be up, I gather. Did you also have east wing duty on the day Mr. Camden was killed?"

Rosalia had relaxed somewhat, but at the mention of the murder she looked frightened again. However, she managed a quick nod. Reluctantly, she then described her morning activities of that day. This time Mr. Applebee's breakfast order had been waffles, and again he was the only person who had ordered the meal to be sent to his room. Rosalia had seen neither Dr. Ronnquist leave for his bird-watching nor Mr. Camden going to practice putting. That morning she swept the stairs between the ground and second floor while waiting for her beeper to go off in order to carry the tray to the writer's suite.

The only person the maid saw during that time was Andi going toward the east wing door. Moments later she noticed her come back and run down the hall in the direction of the main building. Having finished sweeping, she thought that surely the gentleman's breakfast should be ready by now. However, the buzzer never went off. Later, she heard sirens and then went to the main building where people were standing around in the hallway, trying to find out what was wrong. Soon Mrs. Garcia came and told her to go back to work.

Rosalia sighed with relief when the lady detective told her, "I have no more questions. You've been very helpful. Thank you."

After the maid had left, Huber pondered what she had learned from her. The culprit must have put the goggles under the domed cover on Applebee's breakfast tray during the short time it was sitting on the alcove. Roughly four to six minutes, Rosalia had guessed. That early in the morning, anyone could have done so unobserved, Regula mused. Then she thought about Mr. Camden's murder. If the maid was telling the truth - - and why shouldn't she? - - the only person she saw that morning was Andi going out the east wing door and re-entering it shortly afterwards. Huber knew that this was when Andi had first learned about the bludgeoning from Dr. Ronnquist. So Mr. Camden as well as the doctor must have left the house before Rosalia went to the patrons' boxes looking for breakfast orders. Unless, of course, she happened to be on the second floor at the time and missed seeing either one going outdoors. That also applied to the villain if he was not using the main entrance or the west wing door to get out.

Frustrated, Regula cried out, "This is not getting me anywhere!" and dashed out of the suite.

Chapter 46

Meanwhile, Emma Demitris stood in front of her students, giving tips on how best to accomplish a quick change of garments during a fashion show. Outwardly she kept going with her spiel, but her inner self dwelled elsewhere. She thought, even if Optimum House survived this major crisis, it would never be the same again. Iris tried not to show it, but with each additional student who pulled out, her spirit suffered another blow. Doubtless the clients and patrons would be leaving soon as well. Jeffrey's murder and the possibility of her prosperous business collapsing had made Iris a broken woman. Emma knew that her employer had recently had an affair but was positive that the woman still loved her husband. Or was it all an act?

"So class, even though there are helping hands backstage, each model is responsible for her own - -"

Emma could not remember where she was going with her lecture and stopped in mid-sentence. All students' eyes seemed to hang on her lips, waiting for her to finish the statement. She was at a total loss, not able to recall her last words.

She finally continued, "Well, you all know the rest." Then she checked her watch and proclaimed, "Class dismissed."

On their way out the door Cyrilla nudged Andi and murmured, "Our esteemed principal is losing it!"

Chapter 47

The putting green looked harmless enough on that Monday afternoon, four days after it had become a crime scene. Members of the Big Bear Lake City Sheriff's Department, with the help of their San Bernardino colleagues, had finished gathering evidence at the scene, and the crime tape had been removed. Once again, the green appeared as tranquil and innocent as it had before Thursday morning.

Regula stood on the green, trying to picture the killing. There were nine practice holes scattered on the lawn with short flags sticking out of each. She stood in the middle of the green for a few minutes, keeping very still. Then she shook her head and deduced that the way the crime had been presented to her just didn't make sense. Next, she walked over to the shed and looked inside. A few putters were leaning against one wall and two boxes of new balls sat on a small table, no larger than a TV tray. She studied the putters briefly and then told herself, but he supposedly was struck down with the club he was using at the time!

Choosing one of the putters and a ball, she went back to the edge of the green and from that distance aimed at one of the holes. She overshot it, and it took three more strokes for the ball to finally drop into the hole. Huber tried to better her score at some of the other holes, but without much success. This green was not as easily conquered as she had expected.

After returning the putter and ball to the shed, she surveyed the entire area once more and concluded, no, I don't buy that he was killed with his own putter. Then

she turned around and walked briskly back towards the
building. Time for the next interview, she thought.

Chapter 48

Moments later, Huber was talking with Emma Demitris. The principal of the modeling school had knocked at her door promptly at 4:15. Everything about this woman was immaculate, with not as much as a hair out of place, Regula thought.

She started by saying, "Mrs. Camden told you who I am and what I'm here for and also about Andi, correct?"

"Only this morning," Mrs. Demitris replied. "Frankly, I am offended that she didn't confide in me earlier."

"I can understand that, but she might have done so for your own protection."

"Maybe. In any event, I told Iris that I can't see what you can possibly accomplish better than the police, but as she wants me to, I'll answer your questions."

"I appreciate that."

After a pause Emma continued, "I should have been suspicious of Andi, but I simply thought that the girl was just a little rough around the edges. Nothing that couldn't be corrected with a little effort. I still feel that she has model potential, but that is irrelevant now."

Then Huber said, "Let's talk about the misdeeds that occurred before Mr. Camden's homicide. Have you formed an opinion as to what those thefts and pranks were about?"

Mrs. Demitris replied, "At first I thought that one or several of my students amused themselves by playing silly tricks. My alarm clock was one of the first items taken. I was astonished that any of them had had the nerve to sneak into my room at night while I was asleep. As the thefts and malicious deeds continued, I changed my mind and rejected the idea that the modeling students had anything to do with it. Now I wonder if these actions are connected to Jeffrey's murder."

Huber nodded. Then she wanted to hear Mrs. Demitris's account of Thursday morning. The principal's recollection of the facts tallied with the information given by Andi. The young woman had woken her up and informed her of the brutal killing. Then they had gone to the Camdens' suite together to awaken Iris, trying their best to break the news to her gently. She had then taken her friend and employer to the kitchen, where Mr. Jimenez poured some brandy for her. When the police arrived, some color had returned to Iris's face and she wanted to see Jeffrey. Mrs. Demitris did not think this a good idea and was glad the deputy sheriff had stopped her.

Then Regula said, "I can see that you are a great help and support to Mrs. Camden during this difficult time."

"I do what I can to ease her burden."

"You have known one another for a long time?"

"Yes, ever since our modeling days."

"And about seven years ago you asked your friend for a teaching position in the school."

"You've got that wrong, Mrs. Huber. Iris was the one who made me a job offer. She was in the process of adding the health clients program and couldn't handle the school on her own any longer."

"Oh, I must have misunderstood." Then she continued, "I heard that you and Mr. Camden used to date before he met Mrs. Camden."

"That's right." And she added, "Iris surely went overboard with information about the past."

"She did not tell me; I learned that fact from Andi."

"Really? How did Andi know?"

"She was chatting with Mr. Camden one day and he told her."

Emma raised an eyebrow and said, "Now, that really surprises me. Jeffrey was a private person, bordering on shy. I always thought that he was still embarrassed about dumping me for Iris, even after all these years. Andi must be extremely good at her job if she got something this personal out of him."

"But you had no ill feelings?"

"Of course I was mad at the time when he dropped me like a hot potato the instant he saw Iris, but I got over it and soon afterwards fell in love with my ex."

"So you held no grudge against Mr. Camden?"

"After so many years? You've got to be kidding!"

"And you must have forgiven Mrs. Camden a long time ago as well."

Emma smiled and replied, "Actually, I was never really angry at her. She can't help herself."

Huber asked, "What do you mean?"

"Surely you must have noticed the effect Iris has on people, especially men."

"Oh, that. Yes, I'm aware that Mrs. Camden has a certain magnetism."

"I'm positive she doesn't do it on purpose; it just happens."

"You might be right about that."

Regula couldn't think of anything else to ask the principal and concluded the interview.

Left alone, she wondered if Emma Demitris, like so many others, had fallen victim to the spell cast by the first lady of Optimum House.

Chapter 49

After Jeffrey Camden's murder and Troy's allergy attack the atmosphere had been glum in the dining hall at every meal. Conversations were kept to a minimum and in hushed voices. Now, four days later, people tried to make an effort at getting back to a sense of normality. Granted, that was only on the surface. Underneath, everyone was wondering who the killer could be and what would happen next.

Except for the two young men, all of the modeling students were present, even the ones who were about to quit the school. These girls hadn't been questioned by the police yet and were waiting for their parents' arrival. Every health-program client was there except Troy, and at the round table the teaching staff was in full force. Huber sat among the patrons, with Iris Camden next to her on the right and an empty chair to her left. None of the patrons was absent. Even Adam Applebee made a rare appearance for dinner that evening.

Valencia Kirkland leaned over the vacant seat between her and Regula and asked, "You're not from the press, are you?"

"No, I'm not a reporter."

Valencia gave her a questioning glance but got no more information out of the new guest. Then she whispered, "The empty chair was Jeffrey's. It gives me the creeps to look at it. I wonder why Iris told us to leave it vacant?"

"That's my fault. I asked Mrs. Camden to keep it unoccupied," Regula replied.

Again the actress gave her an inquiring stare, but was again left without an explanation. Iris had introduced the newcomer simply as R.A. Huber to the people at her table, giving no other information about the lady. The actress was the only one who was curious, though. The other patrons did not show the slightest interest in the new guest. Brant Ronnquist and Adam Applebee both seemed absent minded, and Chad Richmond devoted his entire attention to Iris.

Isandro had created another sensational meal. The minced meat looked and tasted like veal but was in fact turkey. It was served in a curry sauce over wild rice and garnished with green beans. For dessert there was fresh fruit, pineapple for the students and grapefruit for the clients; and of course the patrons were welcome to have either, or both.

As people were about to leave, Mrs. Camden stood up and said, "May I have everyone's attention? Please remain in your seats for another few minutes. Mrs. Huber here would like to address all of you."

Regula got to her feet and began, "My name is R.A. Huber and I'm a private investigator." She looked at her audience. For the most part she saw surprise and doubt in people's faces. Some looked enthusiastic and seemed eager to hear what she had to say, while others appeared indifferent.

She continued, "A little less than three weeks ago Mr. and Mrs. Camden hired me to find the person responsible for the transgressions at Optimum House. I decided to plant my assistant among you to evaluate the situation."

She paused dramatically and then looked over to the students' table and beckoned, "Come, Andi, I reserved you a seat next to me."

"Yes, ma'am," the latter said, and got up.

The students raised exclamations of surprise and disbelief, and all eyes in the room followed Andi as she walked over to the patrons' table.

The lady detective proceeded, "Andi was not idle; she gathered lots of facts and periodically reported to me. I can honestly say that we are making progress with the case. Now that we're dealing with not only thefts and spiteful deeds but two murders and a possible attempted murder, Andi and I will work around the clock and leave no stone unturned until we find the criminal."

Huber noticed a hand up in the air and said, "Yes?"

Susie stammered, "You said two murders! Who else got killed?"

"It is probable that the maid Lupe did not drown by accident."

There was total silence in the room as this piece of news sank in.

"Now then, let me continue. We will interview all of you, one at a time, starting tomorrow morning. If any of you know or suspect something about the thefts and misdeeds or the murders and Troy's allergy attack, I urge you to come forward before then. I'll be in my suite all evening. In the meantime, I would like to stress that you all need to be extremely careful and on your guard. There is a ruthless killer in our midst and - -"

Without warning, all the lights went out, leaving the dining hall engulfed in total darkness. Someone yelled "Earthquake!" as people screamed and panicked, and soon there was chaos. Chairs were pushed aside while some automatically ducked under tables and others were trying to find their way out of the place and bumped into one another. Somebody shouted, "God help us, we'll all be killed!"

Huber's commanding voice drowned out all other sounds, "Everyone stays where they are! No one is to move." People seemed shocked into obedience.

Then she said, "Maybe a circuit breaker tripped or Big Bear is experiencing a blackout, but let's make certain. Andi, go try and turn the lights on."

"Yes, ma'am."

Andi stopped to think where the nearest switches were located and then crawled on her hands and knees in the approximate direction of the ones on her side of the room. She knew that she had reached the wall when she bumped her head into it. Then she straightened up and moved along the wall, feeling for the light switches. She found one of the six toggle switches and flipped it on, then pushed up the others. Sure enough, the florescent ceiling lights came back on. Everyone sighed with relief, and the people who had taken cover under the tables scurried to their feet.

Huber scrutinized everyone in the room. Nobody seemed hurt, and as far as she could judge, all were present. She stared at each person in turn.

Then she finally said, "I'm in no mood for practical jokes," picked up her purse from under the table, and walked out the door.

Chapter 50

Andi said, "Well, boss, what was that all about?"

"I wish I knew," Huber replied.

They sat on the sofa in Regula's suite, and Andi went on, "You don't really think some idiot pulled a practical joke, do you?"

"No, we are definitely past considering pranks or jokes. There has got to be a reason for this evening's episode, but I cannot come up with anything that makes sense." Then she asked, "How many light switches are there on that wall?"

"Six; two rows of three."

"Are they close together?"

"Pretty close. Why do you want to know?"

"The lights were not turned off individually; they all went out at once."

Andi took a moment to think and then said, "If the person used both hands, he or she could've flipped all the switches down at the same time."

"There are other light switches in the room than the ones you went to, I presume?"

"There is a set at the other end of the room."

"Also with six toggle switches?"

"Yes, ma'am."

Huber nodded and said, "Everyone stayed in their seats during my speech, as far as I can tell. I didn't have a direct view to the switches near us, but I think I'd have noticed movement in that direction out of the corner of my eye. I certainly didn't see anyone going to the light switches at the far end of the room. Did you?"

Andi shook her head.

"Yet someone obviously did reach one of the switches." Then she asked, "So what did you make of the expressions on people's faces when I informed everyone of your role?"

"Well, boss, I'm kinda disappointed. I mean, some of my fellow students looked mad, especially Cyrilla was pissed off, but I expected that. I was hoping to see worry, alarm, guilt or something, but I didn't see any of that."

"I agree. There was surprise registered on most faces and eagerness in a few, but I didn't detect fear of being discovered in a single one."

Then she said, "I had a clear view of the students and clients, and I glanced at the people sitting at my table, but I didn't get a good look at the staff, since they sat to the side and behind me. Did you happen to notice the reactions of Mrs. Brackenbury and Ms. Dugat when I suddenly announced that you'd been placed here as my employee? I'm not concerned with Mrs. Demitris; she already knew about you ahead of time."

Andi considered this and then said, "Mrs. Brackenbury had on her usual poker face, and Ms. Dugat looked amused."

"So we didn't accomplish much in the dining hall, except provoke someone to turn off the lights and frighten people."

Andi stated, "And most people were scared out of their wits. The person who hollered 'Earthquake!' totally lost it. Earthquake, my foot; nothing was shaking."

"I think that the perpetrator was that person and yelled it to make people panic, but why?"

They did not speak for a while, each following her own train of thought.

Suddenly Regula got up and disappeared into the bedroom. Seconds later she came back, waving her purse in the air, saying, "I can tell you the reason for the blackout! The purpose of the entire show was to steal my pistol. Why on earth didn't I think of that right away? I felt someone next to my legs in the dark, but assumed Valencia Kirkland was crouching under the table in fear of an earthquake."

Andi stared. Then she asked, "You carried the piece in your handbag?"

Huber nodded and said, "Turning off the lights was a diversion so that the culprit could crawl under the table and lift my gun out of the purse." And after a pause she added, "How did the person even know that I kept it there? The whole thing still doesn't make sense."

"You think the criminal is gonna use the gun to kill some more?"

"Should prove difficult without ammunition."

"It's unloaded?"

"Yes. For safety reasons I don't carry my pistol around loaded, unless I feel threatened or need to make a citizen's arrest."

Andi chuckled. "Must've been a blow to the murderer when he found out the gun had no bullets in it!" Then she got serious again and said, "How did he smuggle the piece out of the dining hall, I wonder? Except for you, Mrs. Huber, no one ever brings a purse to dinner. A shopping bag or container would draw attention, and to carry the piece on one's person leaves a bulge."

"You are right, of course. I suspect that the culprit hid it somewhere in the dining hall and then retrieved it later."

"Want me to go look for it, boss?"

"Don't bother. Our criminal is too smart to wait this long. He must assume that I have already discovered the loss."

Then she abruptly jumped up and ran to the bathroom. Seconds later Andi heard her exclaim, "Oh no!" and went to see what the problem was. She found her boss staring into a makeup case in disbelief.

Huber looked up, anxiety evident in her face, as she stated, "My ammunition is gone! Now we have a killer running around with a loaded gun!"

Chapter 51

Cyrilla was listening to music and ignored her room-mate when she entered.

Andi said, "I don't blame you for being mad at me."

The former did not reply and turned her music up louder.

Andi stepped over to the DVD system and turned it off. Then she said, "We need to talk."

Cyrilla's stare was hostile as she exploded, "I thought we were friends. Turns out you're nothing but a dirty spy! I trusted you with my secret, but you kept yours to yourself."

"I know I've hurt your feelings, but I couldn't let you in on why I'm here. Can't you understand?"

Cyrilla didn't answer, but continued with what was on her mind. "I should've known when you showed up riding a motorcycle! I thought you were just a little wild and needed coaching. Well, I gave you some good laughs, I'm sure."

Andi said solemnly, "I appreciate everything I've learned from you."

"All that stuff about growing up in Louisiana and your daddy dying was all lies. I bet you were born and raised right here in California and your accent is fake."

"Everything I told you about my background is the gospel truth. Making you think that I was interested in becoming a model was the only dishonest thing I did to you."

By this time Cyrilla had vented her anger and seemed calmer. She asked, "Did you tell that investigator of yours about me?"

"If you mean the sex change and all, the answer is, of course not. I promised I'd keep it to myself!"

Cyrilla switched back to her normal good humor and wanted to know, "So tell me, girl, how's your sleuthing coming along, then?"

"I'm working hard at it," Andi replied with a grin.

"I guess you're moving to investigating headquarters and I'm getting my room back to myself?"

"You're outta luck; I like it here and I'm staying."

After a pause Cyrilla said, "Well, girl, looks like neither of us is going to New York."

"I'm not," said Andi, "but in your case, where there's a will, there's a way!"

Chapter 52

Next evening, Regula called home to keep Peter abreast of the happenings at Big Bear Lake. When she told him about the theft of her pistol and ammunition, he was concerned, to say the least.

He said, "I don't like this one bit. I'm sure you're aware that this is turning into an extremely dangerous situation. Please take precautions and be on your guard. I'm sure the killer wouldn't hesitate to use the pistol on you, if provoked."

"Oh, I'm careful and so is Andi; you really don't need to worry. I aim to find my pistol and the criminal before someone else gets hurt."

"So the gun was taken out of your purse during the blackout. What about your ammunition?"

"The only times I was out of the suite yesterday was during lunch and the 20 minutes or so when I checked out the putting green. Everyone except the domestic help was present in the dining hall after dinner. I'm not considering any of the domestics as the culprit, by the way. The criminal must have stolen the ammunition first and the pistol second, which doesn't make sense."

"Why not?"

"Would anyone come into my suite planning to steal bullets without having a gun to go with it? That seems idiotic, and this murderer is by no means stupid, I'm sure of that."

After a pause he suggested, "Maybe he wasn't looking for anything in particular and was just snooping. Then, when he found the ammunition, he searched for a gun. When he couldn't find it in your suite, he guessed that you might carry it in your purse and so planned his lights-out heist."

"Peter! You're a genius! That is what must have happened."

Then he said, "So what did you do today?"

"I talked to a slew of people and Andi sat in on the conversations. She's sharp and a great help. Sometimes she thinks of additional questions to ask the suspects, things I wouldn't think of. Anyhow, we talked to the 12 high-school-age students first since some of them are leaving this evening. The authorities questioned them today too, in the presence of their parents. Then we interviewed the two male students and their teacher, and four of the health-program clients so far. None of these people could tell us anything that we didn't already know. I'm counting on a more productive day tomorrow with the rest of the students and clients, as well as the teaching staff and patrons."

"Did the police question you?"

"Not yet, and maybe they won't. After all, I only got here yesterday and cannot be considered as a suspect. Mrs. Camden informed them about Andi and me, and they did interview Andi."

They ended the call but not before Peter stressed the danger factor to his spouse once more.

Chapter 53

As soon as the door closed behind Roland Wempel on Wednesday morning, Andi exclaimed, "We're getting nowhere!"

Regula nodded and said, "Mr. Wempel was cooperative, but he didn't tell us anything new."

"Go figure! Of all the folks we've talked to, not one person saw who walked over to the light switches on Monday evening."

"That's understandable. Most eyes were on me while I gave my little speech."

"Guess so." Then Andi asked, "Who's next?"

"Mrs. Parsall. We might as well get all the clients out of the way."

When Paula Parsall walked into the suite, she first looked grimly at Andi and shook her finger back and forth. Then she tossed her curly dark head, walked to the sofa and sat down.

Before Huber got a chance to start the questioning, Paula addressed her, "I've got no idea who killed Mr. Camden, and it's driving me crazy. I usually figure out what goes on in a place, but here I'm at a loss." And before anyone uttered a word, she went on, "I could think of a couple of people I wouldn't mind murdering myself, but Mr. Camden? He was totally harmless, and to think that now he can't even enjoy all that money."

She took a breath, and the private investigator quickly asked, "Who deserves to be murdered, in your opinion?"

"Oh, that was just a manner of speech. I don't like Valencia Kirkland and am not a fan of Applebee either."

"Why is that?"

"Valencia is full of herself. The other day I was just about to get a haircut when she waltzed in and demanded to have her roots done right away. The beautician dropped everything and took care of her first. I mean, just because she's a patron and a famous actress doesn't give her the right to push people around. She's not even a good actress, if you ask me." And looking over at Andi she said, "Now you, my dear, are an excellent one. I don't get easily taken, but you had me fooled!"

She continued, "As for Adam Applebee, the man is antisocial. He snubbed me when I tried to talk to him. I'll definitely never buy any of his books. Granted, Mrs. Camden makes a point of 'giving the patrons privacy,' as she puts it, but what's the harm in a friendly word or two?" She laughed heartily as she recalled, "I was having a heyday when I pictured the goggles being served to him for breakfast! Now, with the murder and Troy's terrible attack, the situation has become serious."

"I agree with you there," Regula remarked. Then she said, "I understand that you found Mrs. Demitris's alarm clock in your room after it was stolen, correct?"

Paula nodded and said, "I'm here to lose weight and was offended that the villain placed it on my scale. No need to rub it in."

"I'm sure if you had any idea who that villain was, you'd have come forward and said so long ago?"

"I've tried to figure out who sneaked into my room ever since it happened, but without any luck. The alarm clock was left there at lunch time, so just about anyone could've done it."

"Now let's get to the morning when Mr. Camden was killed. What is your recollection about that?"

"I'd just come out of the shower when I heard sirens. So I quickly threw on my robe and hurried to the main building to see what was the matter. When I got there, people were standing around in the hallway all talking at once. No one seemed to know what was going on. Somebody said that whatever the trouble might be, it was happening at the putting green since the police seemed headed that way. I started for the main door, but the housekeeper stopped me. Determined to go to the putting green and ferret out what was going on, I walked down the corridor and planned to exit by the east wing door."

Winking at Andi, she continued, "The supposed 'new student' with flaming hair didn't let me out that door either. So I walked back to join the crowd in the hallway again."

"Who was there?"

"Oh, pretty much everyone. Most students, I would think, and I saw people from our group. Some of the maids lingered too, until the housekeeper told them to go back to work. I didn't see Dr. Ronnquist or Valencia Kirkland, but Applebee was standing around in slippers and bathrobe with his skinny white legs sticking out like toothpicks. The new patron was there; I can't remember his name at the moment. Speaking of which, I finally figured out with whom Iris Camden is having an affair."

She took time out to breathe and then went on, "Mrs. Brackenbury made all the students leave, and Ms. Dugat told us to go to our rooms, or have breakfast, or whatnot. She didn't get rid of me that easily; I demanded to get news about what had happened. Then the deputy sheriff came in through the main entrance and told us to go into the dining hall until further notice. I didn't dare argue with him and was on my way there when Mrs. Camden and Mrs. Demitris came out of the kitchen. Mrs. Camden looked awful, and I knew something terrible must have happened. She cried out, 'Let me go to Jeffrey,' but the deputy held her back. I realized then that Mr. Camden must have gotten hurt, but hadn't the faintest idea he was actually murdered until later when the sheriff came into the dining hall and told us."

Andi was thankful for the brief silence that followed. The woman's non-stop chatter had nearly put her to sleep. She glanced at her boss, but Mrs. Huber seemed to have paid close attention and looked interested. So Andi pulled herself together, sat up straight, and forced her mind back to the interview.

Huber asked, "Did I hear you say that Mrs. Camden is having an affair?"

"That's right. I knew for some time that she has a lover, but not who it was. Now I know that it is the new patron."

"Who told you that?"

"Nobody, but there is no mistaking what goes on in his mind when he looks at her."

"Interesting! What can you tell me about the incident after dinner the other night? Did you by chance see anyone walk over to the light switches?"

"No, I was looking at you."

"You mentioned something about money where Mr. Camden was concerned. What was that all about?"

"It's no secret that Mr. Camden inherited a fortune when his father died last year."

"I see." And after a pause she said, "I think we covered everything, or do you have more questions, Andi?"

"Just one, please, Mrs. Parsall. The first time you and I talked, you told me personal stuff about the people here. How did you know all that?"

Smiling, she replied, "You don't seriously think I'd give away my source," and got up to leave.

Chapter 54

"Yap, yap, yap. How that woman loves to talk," Andi commented when Paula was out the door.

Huber said, "Why did you ask that last question?"

"I wanted to find out which of her gossip was true. Looks like none of it was. She's such a blabbermouth that if any of that stuff was on the level, she would've mentioned who told her."

"Not necessarily. Despite her obvious pleasure in gabbing, the lady seems to know when to hold her tongue." Then she asked, "So have we learned anything new from her?"

"You think she was telling the truth about Mr. Camden being loaded?"

"Probably. I doubt that she has the nerve to make anything like that up under the circumstances."

"What about the affair between Mrs. Camden and Chad Richmond? You reckon that's so?"

"Your guess is as good as mine," Regula replied.

Susie Seales stuck her head in and said, "Am I too early?"

Huber beckoned, "No, no, come in, please."

As she walked into the room, the bubbly young woman looked admiringly at Andi and said, "When you came here, I thought you had nothing else on your mind than becoming a model like the rest of us. Little did I know that I would actually end up befriending a private eye!" She giggled, rubbed her hands together and exclaimed, "Oh, this is so exciting!"

As Susie plopped herself down on the couch, Huber stated, "This is not a game, Ms. Seales."

"Oh, I know. That's why I admire Andi so much. I'd never have the courage to solve murder cases and get myself into dangerous situations like I'm sure you are both up against."

Regula smiled and said, "Our job is not always exciting. It involves the tedious task of questioning the suspects, as you'll find out in a moment when it's your turn."

Susie's eyes widened as she asked, "You consider me a suspect?"

"Certainly. In my eyes everyone is a suspect until proven otherwise."

And so the talk began. Like all the other people questioned so far, Susie Seales had not much to contribute. She had not seen or heard anything pertinent to either the misdeeds or the killings. On the morning of Mr. Camden's murder, she came downstairs when she heard sirens and then stood in the hallway with everyone else until Mrs. Brackenbury told the students to disperse. When asked about the evening of the blackout, she stated that she had not seen anyone turning off the lights.

After Susie had left, Andi remarked, "It ain't an act; she's always that cheerful."

Chapter 55

"In what order are you tackling the students?" Andi wanted to know.

"No special order. As soon as a modeling student returns to class, Mrs. Demitris sends the next one over."

"You mind if I don't sit in on Cyrilla's interview?"

"No problem. Is she still angry at you, then?"

"We talked it out and I think she's forgiven me."

"But?"

"We're kinda close. Guess I feel like a traitor."

The person who entered the suite next was Olivia Volmer, however. R. A. Huber looked the young woman over. She was tall and slender and, although no beauty, made the best of her appearance. The result was an impression of elegance and grace. As soon as she opened her mouth, though, it was all over.

She said in a voice a tad too loud, "Hello, Mrs. Huber." And with an angry glance at Andi, "Good morning to you too, *mole*."

Turning back to Regula, she stated, "I can't imagine who killed Mr. Camden. It certainly wasn't me. We now have one male less and there weren't enough to begin with. Worst of all, I never sneaked under his covers and now it's too late, he's dead!" She eyed the lady sleuth provokingly and asked, "Am I shocking you, Mrs. Huber?"

"At my age, I don't shock easily, Ms. Volmer."

"Did Agent Andi warn you about me?"

Regula looked at the young woman intently and then said, "In my experience, I've found two reasons why a person is preoccupied with the subject of sex. He or she is either a nymphomaniac, or is sexually frustrated. My guess is that you belong in the second category."

Olivia gawked at her, speechless for once.

Then Huber started with her questions. "I understand that your makeup case was taken. Tell me how that came about, please."

"I was using one of the downstairs bathrooms and accidentally left it there. When I went back to look for the case, someone had taken it. I was hopping mad!"

"But then it showed up in Mr. Wempel's backpack. Right?"

"Sure, two days later. By that time I'd already made a special trip to the village to replace the makeup. There is no way that I'd walk around without it."

When Regula inquired about her movements on the morning of Mr. Camden's murder, her answers were basically the same as Susie's a few minutes earlier. As far as Monday evening was concerned, she did not see anyone go over to either location of the light switches in the dining hall.

After Olivia had left, Andi chuckled and said, "*You told her!*" Then she became pensive and added, "I thought that she got out of control when leaving the Catholic boarding school, sort of 'let loose.' Judging by her expression when you nailed her, it looks like she went the other extreme. Think she's a virgin?"

"Most likely."

"So why the big act?"

Regula said, "In my day, staying a virgin until marriage was considered a virtue. Now, young women tend to be ashamed of the fact."

"So why doesn't she just get laid and get it over with?"

"I suppose that she would like to be promiscuous and wants others to think that she is, but can't bring herself to do so because of her strict Catholic roots."

Chapter 56

Next, Cyrilla Washington glided into the suite. Huber had glimpsed the tall African American beauty from a distance on a couple of occasions. Now, close up, her radiance and the proud, majestic bearing fully came to light.

Andi got to her feet, saying, "Y'all excuse me," and left.

Cyrilla faced the private investigator and declared, "So she's chickened out!"

"I wouldn't put it that way. She felt uncomfortable because this is personal for her."

The young woman didn't seem to understand. Then she suddenly produced a bright smile and said, "Sort of like a cop is never put on a case involving kinfolk?"

"You got it!"

"I was real angry at her, you know."

Huber nodded.

After a pause, Cyrilla remarked, "How anyone prefers sleuthing over becoming a model is beyond me. Did she tell you that Fielding, New York was interested in her?"

"No, that's news to me, although I can't say I'm surprised." Then she felt it was time to get to the point and said, "I heard your dress was cut to shreds and later discovered by a maid."

"That's right, and it was my favorite too."

"Did you know the maid who found it?"

"I don't know any of the maids. Mrs. Garcia came and told me."

Huber said, "Lupe, the domestic who drowned, noticed the destroyed dress in the waste basket. Does that suggest anything to you?"

Cyrilla thought this through and then asked, "You mean she knew who cut it to pieces and was murdered because of it?"

"Possibly."

"I think I'm gonna quit the school and get out of here. I don't like the evil doings going on."

Then Regula asked, "Tell me about your early morning on the day Mr. Camden was killed, please."

"How early?"

"Before seven."

"I was asleep."

"At what time did you wake up?"

"Must've been around 8:30."

"You didn't hear the sirens?"

"Not me."

"You sleep soundly!"

"Like a baby. Ask Andi."

"So when did you learn about Mr. Camden's murder?"

"When I was about to grab a banana and some juice in the dining hall before going to class, Andi told me."

"You had no idea of anything out of the ordinary going on before that time?"

"No, ma'am."

Then Huber posed what had become routine questions. It came as no surprise to her that Cyrilla had nothing to contribute about the two murders, Troy's allergy attack or the lights in the dining hall.

Left alone, Regula checked her watch. Time for lunch, she thought.

Chapter 57

Out of habit, Andi was eating her lunch with the students that day. Regula came to the dining hall considerably later and walked over to the patron's corner. She found only Valencia Kirkland, flanked by Dr. Ronnquist on one side and Chad Richmond on the other, at the table.

Huber pointed to the vacant chair next to Mr. Richmond and asked, "Is this seat for Mrs. Camden?"

"You're welcome to it. Iris is lying down and won't be joining us," he replied. And without any prompting he continued, "She's taking it hard. Not only does she have to deal with the loss of her husband, but many of her students and even some clients are leaving. At this rate, she'll eventually have to close the facility."

"That would be a shame," Regula said, and helped herself to the buffet lunch of soup and salad.

Valencia remarked, "I'm thinking of calling it quits too. I'd like to stay loyal to Iris, but I'm scared."

Dr. Ronnquist, who had silently consumed his food, rose and said, "I'll see you at dinner," and left.

When Regula had finished eating, she looked around the room. Most of the students were gone, including Andi. A couple of clients lingered on, seemingly deep in conversation. She turned her head and looked over to the round table where the teaching staff had sat moments earlier. Now it was empty. Soon Ms. Kirkland excused herself as well, so that only the lady detective and Chad Richmond were left at the patrons' table.

She addressed him and said, "I was going to talk with you later in my suite, but since we seem undisturbed here, how about answering a few questions now?"

He replied, "If it was up to me, I'd tell you to go jump in Big Bear Lake and refuse to talk to you. After all, you're just a private eye with no authority whatsoever." His eyes softened as he continued, "After you abruptly left the dining hall on Monday evening, Iris told us all to cooperate with you. So for her sake, go ahead with your questions."

"I appreciate that, Mr. Richmond." And she began, "Please give me an account of your movements on the morning that Mr. Camden was killed."

He said, "Let's see. I was about to go to breakfast when I heard sirens. At first I didn't think anything of it. My office is located in L.A., so I'm used to hearing them all the time. Then the noise seemed close by and I realized that, whether it was police, firemen or ambulance, the vehicles had stopped right here in the parking lot."

He continued, "As I said, I was on my way to breakfast. When I got into the main building, people were coming from all directions and then congregating in the hallway near the main entrance. No one knew what was going on, and most were excited or frightened as everyone talked at once. As we tried to go out to the parking lot, the housekeeper and your assistant - - at the time I thought she was a student - - came from there and told us we were not allowed out of the building. The housekeeper stood like a dragon guarding the main entrance, and I later heard that your young woman went over to the east wing door and did likewise.

"After a few minutes an officer in sheriff's uniform told us to wait in the dining hall. So we all drifted in that direction. Needless to say, no one was hungry. As I walked by the kitchen, Iris and the principal passed me on their way out. Iris looked devastated, and when I asked what had happened, she didn't answer. I don't think she even saw or heard me."

"Please go on."

"That's basically it. Later, the sheriff came into the dining hall and told us that Jeffrey had been bludgeoned to death on the putting green."

Huber said, "You seem to be on a first name basis with Mr. and Mrs. Camden. Did you know them before you came to Optimum House?"

"Yes, we met in Hawaii and became friends."

"I see." Then she said, "You only arrived recently, so you missed out on the strange happenings that occurred here. Did anyone tell you about them, though?"

"Iris touched on it briefly when I first got here. She seemed upset about it all, so I didn't press her to tell me more."

"Are you in a relationship with Mrs. Camden?"

Chad glared at her and said, "That is none of your business."

"Under the circumstances it could be." Then she went on, "Now, about the other night: Did you see anyone going to either set of light switches just before the blackout?"

"No, I didn't. I was concentrating on you, Mrs. Huber."

"I seem to have had an extremely attentive audience." And she asked, "Did you by any chance notice who ducked under our table as the lights went out?"

"I think Valencia Kirkland did and maybe Adam Applebee, but I'm not sure. I certainly stayed in my seat. The person who shouted 'Earthquake' was crazy; I know all too well what a quake feels like. Why do you ask?"

"Oh, just a little idea of mine. It's of no importance." Then she inquired, "Are you going to stay put, or have you decided to leave us too, Mr. Richmond?"

"I'm not going to abandon Iris in her hour of need," he answered.

Chapter 58

Some fresh air and a little exercise would suit me now, Regula thought when leaving the dining hall. She went outdoors through the main entrance to the parking lot and then walked along the large building. She glanced over to the two-story structure across the lot that housed the domestic help. The larger ground-level apartments each contained a good-sized patio, and the smaller ones upstairs had balconies. The way people kept their porches expressed great individuality. Some were decked out with patio furniture and barbecues while others showcased potted plants and flowers.

Regula came to the end of the east wing building. The path in front of her, which she had taken on Monday, led straight to the putting green. Another wound around the premises. She chose the latter, bringing her to the back of the house where the walkway forked. Heading to the right would have taken her to the pool entrance, but she opted for the trail to her left. She followed the curvy path that led along tall trees and bushes. To her surprise, as she came around the last bend, she faced the putting green, this time from the opposite side. She lingered a moment, shook her head in disbelief once more at the thought of Jeffrey Camden being allegedly killed with his own putter, and then left the green behind.

Andi had described the clearing with the view to the lake, so Huber went in search of it. She chose to hike over the meadows rather than going through the woods. The day was unusually warm for late May with temperatures in the mid eighties. When she had conquered the last stretch, clambering up the short, steep climb, she saw that someone was already sitting on the bench at the edge of the plateau.

The young woman's eyes were focused on the lake. As she was paying close attention to drawing the landscape, she did not hear Huber's approach. A mass of dark, straight hair fell loosely down her back. She was slim with long legs extending from khaki shorts. Even while concentrating on her artwork she had good posture, possibly as a result of her training at the modeling school. Suddenly she looked up, and Regula gazed into a pair of huge brown eyes.

"You're Nancy Zagarian, right?"

She nodded.

"May I join you and ask a few questions?"

"If you must."

The private eye sat down next to her, and Nancy tucked the sketch she was working on into a large folder. They sat quietly for a couple of minutes, admiring the scenery.

Huber remarked, "It sure is peaceful up here!"

"Yes, I love this spot," the young woman replied.

Nancy's account of the events on the morning of Mr. Camden's murder tallied with the recollections of the people Huber had already talked to. She had gathered in the hallway with her peers until Mrs. Brackenbury told them to disperse. When asked if she had known about Troy's allergy to peanuts, she replied in the affirmative. Soon it became clear to the investigator that Nancy was extremely shy. Wherever possible, she gave only yes-or-no answers.

When Regula probed if she had seen anyone going to the light switches on Monday evening, Nancy said, "I was drawing a sketch of you and didn't pay attention."

"Oh! May I see it?"

"I wanted to give it to you that same evening but didn't get the chance."

"Yes, I left the dining hall rather quickly. I'd still like to have a look at it, though."

"It's gone."

"You tossed it?"

"No, someone took it from my folder."

"Tell me how that came about."

"Okay. I always take my folder along wherever I go. The only place I'm not allowed to have it is in the classroom. Early on in the semester, Mrs. Demitris caught me drawing during a theory session and forbade me to take it to class. So I usually leave the folder outside the door. Yesterday morning someone must have taken that sketch while I was in class."

"I see. Was any of your other artwork stolen?"

"No. The person only took the top drawing, which was of you."

"Did you report the theft?"

Nancy shook her head. "With murder going on, I didn't think a missing pencil sketch was important."

"Did you draw any other people in that sketch?"

"I focused on you, but just before the lights went out I added some background."

"With persons in it?"

"Not really. Just shadows of people sitting at your table and the round one."

"Anyone recognizable?"

"Oh no, nothing precise. Just a few pencil strokes."

Then Huber said, "Now let's talk about the Barbie and Ken exhibit. I understand you discovered the two dolls in the hallway display case in what seemed a lynched position."

She nodded.

"Was this extremely noticeable, then?"

She shrugged and explained, "I walked past that case every day on my way to class without really looking at it, if you know what I mean."

"Yes, I think I do."

"That morning, something different about the display caught my eye. I stopped and saw that Barbie and Ken were actually hanging from the swing cross bar with a piece of yarn around their necks. It was creepy."

"So you sounded the alarm and told Mrs. Camden about it?"

"No, I didn't."

"Whom did you tell, then?"

"Nobody."

"You must have told someone; it is common knowledge that you discovered the two dolls hanging by their necks."

Nancy said, "I was standing in front of the showcase and drew a sketch of the scene. Mrs. Demitris came by and looked over my shoulder while I was working on the drawing. She let out a horrified cry and then said that she didn't think this was funny and that Mrs. Camden needed to be told about the malicious deed. She apparently did tell her, because a little later both of them came back and stared at the morbid scene in the showcase. By that time I was done with the sketch and left."

Making this long speech had taken a great effort on the part of this student. Evidently, she preferred to express herself with pencil and paper rather than words.

Regula asked, "Do you still have the drawing?"

She nodded and rummaged through her folder. "Here it is," she said and handed it over.

Regula surveyed the artwork carefully and then stated, "Yes, definitely a disturbing sight." And after a pause, "May I borrow this for a couple of days?"

"No problem."

Then she looked at the young woman kindly, saying, "You don't really want to become a model, do you?"

"No, but Mom wants me to."

"You're an excellent artist, so follow your instinct."

Chapter 59

As Dr. Ronnquist left the dining hall that Wednesday after lunch, he was mulling over something that seemed to disturb him more and more. He thought, why put on a robe? He had asked himself that question many times without arriving at a reasonable answer. Yet there had to be an explanation. While talking to the police, the robe business hadn't occurred to him yet. It wasn't until a few days later, when he had reflected on every little detail about the morning of the killing, that the thing hadn't made sense to him. Should he now seek the sheriff out and tell him? Maybe that woman investigator, Mrs. Huber, would be a better choice?

He shook his head as he mused, I came here to relax and forget about my troubles, only to be mixed up in a brutal murder case. Then he thought, I was on the verge of overthrowing my demons, dwelling less and less on the miserable event in the operating room, and now this! His mind returned to the dilemma he faced. Then he suddenly came to a decision and told himself, I know what I'm going to do! Why not talk to the person? It surely wouldn't hurt to ask. There has got to be a simple explanation, and jumping the gun by running to either the police or the woman sleuth would make me look like a fool. My mind is made up. I'm going straight to the source of my worries and get an answer.

For the time being, the surgeon managed to ban the homicide and all other unpleasant thoughts from his mind. He stopped at his suite to fetch a small bottle of water and the binoculars, went out the east wing door and walked briskly in the direction of the woods.

Chapter 60

Regula went to the main building and then walked down the hall to have another look at Mrs. Camden's Barbie doll collection. She had seen it on her first day at Optimum House but needed to refresh her memory.

The showcase was approximately four feet long with two shelves, one at eye level and the other below. The exhibit was behind glass, and on the lower shelf one could view Barbie dolls adorned in different outfits. These dolls were arranged according to their manufacturing dates, starting with the oldest of 1959 all the way to the most recent.

The top shelf was cleverly set up by themes. There was Barbie at camp, Barbie by the sea, Barbie goes to Paris with an Eiffel tower in the background, Barbie the pilot, and so forth. The motif at the center of that shelf was Barbie's patio party. The doll was sitting on a swing gazing up at Ken, who was standing beside her. In the background, other dolls were displayed in a group. The impression was that of a couple engaged in an idyllic moment at a party.

Regula thought this was a different picture by far from what she had seen in Nancy's drawing. Then she tried the glass case sliding door, and sure enough, it moved aside for easy access to the shelves. Like everything else at this place, the showcase was kept unlocked.

Chapter 61

Two hours later, Adam Applebee, the last of the suspects interviewed that afternoon, left R.A. Huber's suite. Before him, she and Andi had talked to Mrs. Brackenbury and Ms. Dugat, as well as Valencia Kirkland.

Andi exploded, "Shit! We've tackled all of them and nobody told us a thing!"

Regula replied, "We haven't seen Brant Ronnquist yet. The good doctor is somewhere in the woods chatting with birds."

"I'm counting on a tip-off from him. I reckon he was the only person out and about as early as Mr. Camden, aside from the murderer. He also found the corpse." And she added, "Unless he's the killer, of course."

"That reminds me, tell me again about the murder scene you came upon. Try to remember every detail."

Andi reflected for a second and then began, "When I got to the green I first saw Dr. Ronnquist and told him that I had called 911 and had given Mrs. Camden the bad news. Then I looked behind him where Mr. Camden lay in a bloody mess with many head wounds. His putter lay a few feet from his body, and as I came closer I noticed blood on it. It was Mr. Camden's own club someone used to bludgeon him to death."

She shivered and went on, "I'll never forget the horror; sure made me feel sick. Then I pulled myself together and asked the doctor if there was any chance Mr. Camden was alive. He said that the man had been dead for at least 30 minutes. When we heard the sound of sirens coming from the highway, Dr. Ronnquist said he'd stay with the body and sent me to the parking lot to wait for the police and direct them to the putting green."

Huber said, "Yes, that is exactly what I tried to picture when I heard it the first time, but I just don't buy it. Are you sure that the bloody putter was Mr. Camden's and not one taken out of the shed?"

"Yes, ma'am, I'm sure it was his. He showed it to me one morning when I stopped at the putting green to chat with him. He had it custom made for himself. Why is that bothering you?"

"Remember, you said that in your opinion the high school girls were not strong enough to attack Mr. Camden?"

"Yeah?"

"Well, I think that goes for everybody else as well. Mr. Camden was a big, powerful man despite his injury. It stands to reason that he held his putter when the murderer approached him, and I can't believe that anyone was able to take it away from him."

Andi replied, "I reckon you're right. I've seen Mr. Camden working out in the gym, and he was strong, no arguing that."

"Do you know if the officers are still on the premises?"

"I didn't see them today. What's on your mind, boss?"

"I'd like to know if it is a fact that Mr. Camden's golf club was the murder weapon. They might not tell me, of course." And she added, "I should talk to them anyhow and report the theft of my pistol."

Then she asked, "So what have we learned from the last four people we questioned?"

"Zilch!"

"You're wrong there. Mrs. Brackenbury, for instance, was the first and only person who asked if we had news about Troy."

"So?"

"That could mean she was truly concerned about the boy's well-being, or she was fishing for information about his whereabouts."

"Oh!"

"With Valencia Kirkland one is never sure what her true feelings are. The lady is always 'on stage.'"

Andi commented, "I've noticed."

"She clearly wanted to evade the subject when I asked if she'd ever been married to someone by the name of Camden. Still, she at least volunteered his first name."

"How did you know that one of her husbands was a Camden?"

"I usually don't keep track of celebrities' personal lives, but I vaguely remember reading something in the paper years ago about a fatal accident of one of her spouses. As I was looking at the actress this afternoon, I suddenly recalled that the man's name was Camden."

Andi said, "I wonder if Dwayne Camden was the guy that Paula Parsall was talking about."

"Oh, that's right. She told you about some scandal concerning Valencia Kirkland. Tell me about that."

Andi responded sadly, "Sorry, boss. Mrs. Parsall got on my nerves with her chatter, and I didn't listen to half she said."

"Try to recall as best you can, then."

"Something about a boating accident Kirkland's third husband was in. I think she said that he fell overboard and the incident looked suspicious. I'm mighty sorry, Mrs. Huber, but I can't remember more."

"Don't worry about it," Huber said. Then she continued, "Ms. Dugat seems an extremely level-headed individual. Her quick action of collecting Troy's food and drink after his attack was either rational thinking or a calculated act."

"I don't understand."

"If she were the perpetrator, she'd show eagerness to catch the criminal."

Andi thought this over and then said, "I get you now. She'd know that the peanut oil was in the dressing, but it didn't matter if others, like the police, got wise to it. Everyone knew Troy was allergic to the stuff and must've eaten some."

"Exactly."

"What about the writer? I reckon you found something incriminating about him. Beats me what that could be, though!"

Regula smiled and said, "Telling us that he overslept on the morning of Mr. Camden's murder is interesting."

"How come?"

"Here is a man that likes to have his breakfast delivered to him at 7:00, give or take a few minutes. He is also the kind of person who'll make a fuss if his orders are not carried out according to his wishes. So it makes sense that on that morning when his waffles were not brought to him as expected, he would have complained. Yet, the first time Mr. Applebee shows a sign of life is some 30 to 40 minutes later when he gathers at the main building with everyone else, claiming the sound of the sirens had woken him out of a deep sleep."

"Yeah, that's definitely suspicious."

"Or he told the truth and actually overslept."

Andi laughed and said, "And just as I started to think he was our man!" Then she remarked, "Maybe we'd best look at the folks who were fully dressed on the morning of the murder."

"Good idea. You saw most people. Who was dressed?"

"Let me see. That'd be Mrs. Brackenbury, Ms. Dugat, Nancy Zagarian, Mr. Wempel and a couple of other clients, the new patron, the cook and his two assistants, all the maids - - oh, and Dr. Ronnquist, of course." Then she shook her head and went on, "No, I don't think that works. Someone could've gone out to kill Mr. Camden in his or her pajamas."

Huber remarked, "Cyrilla Washington and Valencia Kirkland did not leave their rooms at all during the commotion. Cyrilla claims she slept through it, not hearing a thing and - -"

Andi interrupted, "I can vouch for Cyrilla; she's the soundest sleeper I know."

Regula smiled again and continued, "The statement of Valencia Kirkland that, although awakened by the sirens, she wasn't about to leave her room without proper attire and makeup on, is plausible coming from the actress."

Then she showed the young woman the sketch of the lynched Barbie and Ken.

Andi studied it carefully and then said, "I agree with Cyrilla; there was evil doings going on here way before the murder."

Huber scrutinized the drawing once more and pointed out, "Look at the background. See that first doll behind the swing?"

"Yeah?"

"The doll has her arms outstretched in the direction of the lynched Barbie and Ken. I find that interesting."

"Like saying "Ta – dah!"

"Now, and I assume also before the nasty prank, that doll is displayed with the arms to her sides and standing further back facing a group of others."

They sat in silence for a while, and then Andi asked, "So what do we do now?"

"We consider everything we've learned from each suspect and also the observations you made since you first came here. Then we have another pow-wow and compare notes."

"Sure thing, boss!"

"You may stay here while we meditate or go somewhere else to mull things over."

"I'm going for a swim in the pool; my brain works best when I'm physically active."

As Andi got up to leave, Regula looked at her intently and said, "Please be careful!"

"Yes, ma'am."

Chapter 62

Regula stayed put and applied herself to some serious brainwork.

After what seemed only minutes to the private eye but in fact was close to an hour, she had come to a decision and walked out of her suite.

Iris was sitting at her desk in the administrative office, staring into space. She jumped as the door opened.

"I didn't mean to startle you."

"Oh it's you, Mrs. Huber. I was expecting another parent bursting in here and demanding that her child be released immediately."

Regula said, "I sympathize with you, for these must be extremely trying times."

"The officers seem to be dragging their feet. Are you at least making progress with the investigation?"

"I'm working on it, but I'm puzzled about some information I've gathered and hope you can help me out."

"I'll try."

"Last time we talked, you said that Mrs.Demitris applied for the position at the modeling school, but when I interviewed her she was positive that it was you who had offered the job to her."

"Oh, did Emma say that? I thought it was the other way around. What does it matter anyhow? Whoever's idea, it certainly was a success. Emma is the most reliable and competent principal any school could wish for, and I've come to appreciate her even more these last few days."

"Another thing I'm curious about is why you didn't grant Lupe her wish of being excused from pool duty?"

"What on earth are you talking about?"

"So she didn't come to you and asked to be spared cleaning the pool area because she had a fear of water?"

"Surely not! I told you of being unaware that she couldn't swim. What gave you that idea?"

"Mrs. Garcia was under the impression that Lupe may have come to you with her plea after she denied it to her."

"Well, she didn't."

Regula continued, "I understand that Ms. Kirkland was married to a Dwayne Camden at one time. Was he perchance related to your husband?"

"Dwayne was Jeffrey's older brother."

"I heard that he was killed in a boating accident. Is that correct?"

"Yes, he was."

"Rumor has it that his death may not have been an accident."

Bewildered, Iris said, "Where are you getting your information from, I wonder?" And without waiting for an answer, she continued, "They were cruising the ocean in their yacht. Dwayne fell overboard and drowned. The reason for your rumor is that Valencia didn't report him missing until the next day."

"Why not?"

"I don't remember what they were celebrating, but they both had had way too much to drink. Valencia needed to sober up before calling the authorities."

After a pause Huber asked, "Were the brothers close?"

"Very."

"Did your husband blame Ms. Kirkland for his brother's death?"

"Jeffrey was too nice to ever confront her, but yes, I think he did."

Then Regula inquired, "Why did you put the Barbie and Ken dolls back in the showcase the way they'd been displayed before the morbid hanging? I'd have thought it more natural if you'd removed them from the case altogether."

Absent-mindedly fingering the castle-paperweight Iris replied, "That was my first reaction, but then I thought better of it and said to myself, why let the culprit win? I wanted to show the person that I wouldn't let the sight of the lynched dolls get to me." And she added, "That is far from the truth, for I was deeply disturbed by the scene."

Regula nodded. Then she held her hand out toward the paperweight, saying, "May I?"

Iris handed her the object, and the lady detective admired it at great length. The paperweight resembled a castle out of a storybook fairytale. Its size was about five by four inches with a height of six, if one counted several towers extending from the roof. Weighing it in her palm, she realized that the thing was much heavier than it looked, and she also noticed the sharp edges.

She remarked, "An unusual piece and the craftsmanship is excellent. What is it made of?"

"I believe the artist painted over cast iron."

"That explains the heavy weight," Huber said, and placed it back on the desk. Then she continued, "I hate to bother you with more details about the morning of the murder, but did you go straight to your office after Mr. Jimenez gave you brandy?"

"No. When the officer wouldn't let me go to Jeffrey, I suddenly felt weak. I don't know if it was due to shock or the drink. Emma suggested that I lie down, so I went to my suite. I couldn't really rest, let alone sleep, and was almost glad when the sheriff and his men wanted to question me in my office."

"At what time was that?"

"I have no idea; I didn't look at my watch."

"Did you get here before the police officers, or were they already in the administrative office waiting for you?"

Annoyed, Iris answered, "I don't remember. What difference does it make?"

"Probably none, but I was curious."

Iris eyed the private investigator keenly, but Regula returned her gaze, pokerfaced.

Then the latter said, "That covers all I wanted to know. Thank you for your help. By the way, I need to talk with someone from the Sheriff's Department. Are the officers still around?"

"Not today, and they didn't tell me if or when they'll be back," Iris replied.

Chapter 63

The following day turned into another tragic Thursday at Optimum House. Regula called home that evening with more unsettling news.

Peter said, "Tell me you've solved the case and are calling to let me know you're coming home."

"Not quite. We had another murder today."

"Oh no! Who this time?"

"Dr. Ronnquist, and I fear that he was shot with my pistol."

"Oh Regula! I knew it was bad news when your gun disappeared." Then he said, "Tell me everything that happened."

"Andi and I planned to interview him, only we never got the chance. At dinner last night the doctor agreed to come to my suite after his customary morning of bird-watching. When he failed to show up, we presumed that he got carried away with his hobby and forgot about our meeting. So Andi and I compared notes while we waited.

"We finally went to lunch, figuring we'd catch him in the dining hall. By one o'clock we started to get worried, and half an hour later went on a search. We found him in the wooded area of the estate. He was lying on his side near the pathway with a bullet hole in his back and a couple more in the chest area. The front of his shirt was soaked with dried blood. Dr. Ronnquist was obviously dead, but I attempted to take his pulse anyhow and realized that rigor mortis had started to set in."

"How awful for you," Peter interjected, his voice filled with concern.

"The experience wasn't pleasant," she admitted. "There isn't much else to tell. We called the authorities, and I stayed with the body while Andi went back to the house to wait for the law enforcement officers so she could lead them to the murder scene."

She paused and then continued, "I feel awful about Dr. Ronnquist. If we'd only questioned him yesterday! I probably couldn't have prevented his death, but I might have tried."

"Don't blame yourself, Regula. Do you suppose that he knew something about Mr. Camden's homicide and had to be silenced?"

"I would think so, but whatever it was, I doubt that the doctor felt it was crucial information."

"Why not?"

Regula replied, "He'd have come forward with what he knew, and I also believe that the murderer wouldn't have waited so many days to strike again." As an afterthought she added, "Unless of course the killer was unaware of the man's knowledge until recently."

Then Peter asked, "Did the police question you?"

"Yes. The sheriff wasn't exactly pleased with me for not having reported the theft of my pistol, but - -"

"Why didn't you?"

"I meant to, but hadn't got around to doing so."

"I don't blame him for being annoyed!"

"Don't lecture me, Peter. I heard it all from the sheriff. He spent some time talking about gross negligence, et cetera, et cetera." She went on, "Nevertheless, he was kind enough to tell me that Mr. Camden had first been hit on the back of his head with a sharp object, followed by numerous blows with the putter to his face and side of the head."

"Did that help you any?"

"Yes, I can finally visualize the attack on Mr. Camden. Until I talked with the sheriff, all I knew was that he'd been bludgeoned with his own putter. I found it hard to believe that someone was able to take the club away from such a strong man. Now I can picture the scene: The killer approached Mr. Camden from behind and delivered a blow to the back of his head with a sharp object, causing him to maybe stumble or fall to the ground and let go of the putter. Then the murderer picked up the putter and hit him numerous times over the head with it.

"When I asked him if it was established which stroke caused the actual death, he said that, according to the coroners' findings, the blow to the back of the head most likely rendered him unconscious, and either of the first two hits with the club killed him."

"So the extensive beating that followed was unnecessary?"

"Evidently."

"What does that tell you?"

"The murderer either was acting in uncontrolled fury or wanted to make sure that Mr. Camden was dead beyond any doubt."

Peter asked, "Did they find the object used for the initial attack?"

"No, and I had a suggestion."

"You usually do."

"Are you making fun of me?" Regula wanted to know.

"Not at all. It was just an observation."

His spouse continued, "Anyhow, I suggested the paperweight in the shape of a castle sitting on Mrs. Camden's desk as a possible weapon. The sheriff said he'd have it examined."

"When's the funeral?"

"I understand that Mr. Camden will be cremated as soon as the authorities release his body, and the memorial service is scheduled for Saturday."

"What about today's murder? Is it a fact that the doctor was shot with your gun?"

"I'm afraid it looks that way, but it's not official. A .25 caliber pistol was used, but the police haven't found it yet."

Then Peter remarked, "I assume this second murder complicates things. You'll have to start all over with the investigation."

"Third murder," Regula corrected.

"Oh, that's right; I forgot about the maid."

"As far as starting all over, I don't think this latest tragedy sets me back all that much."

"So you have an idea as to the villain, then?"

"Lots of ideas!"

"But you're not telling?"

"I've got to sort things out in my mind first." Then she asked, "So what's new at home?"

"Sunshine called to remind us about the family get-together a week from Sunday. When I said that I hoped her mom could make it, she wanted to know where you are and then what you are doing in Big Bear."

"Oh boy!"

"Want to hear the sermon?"

"Not really, but go ahead."

"She reproached me for not having better control over you and making you give up the R.A. Huber business. She feels that you're getting too old for the dangerous job and that it's high time you came to your senses and acted like a normal grandmother."

"Oh boy, oh boy!"

"I heard from Ben too. They'll definitely come to the family gathering and wouldn't miss it for the world, he said. Their plane lands at LAX on Saturday, the day before our get-together."

Regula stated, "I'm planning to have this case wrapped up way before then. So tell Sunshine that she can count her old, feeble mother in for attending the family reunion. Also tell her to make sure there will be plenty of easily chewable and digestible foods when she plans the menu!"

After they hung up Regula thought of her family. She had forgotten when Peter first came up with the nickname "Sunshine" for their daughter. Her name was actually Deborah, but one day when she was in one of her testy moods, he jokingly had called her Sunshine and the name had stuck. The get-together would be great fun, she mused. Since Deborah and her family lived in Northern California, they didn't see them nearly enough. They saw even less of their son Ben, his wife and baby; New York was not exactly next-door. She couldn't wait to play with all of her grandchildren. Then she thought, Regula, old woman, get back to the matter at hand and solve these murders.

Chapter 64

On Friday, the day after the shooting of Dr. Brant Ronnquist, Optimum House seemed doomed. Business as usual was no longer an option as the authorities stepped up their investigation. The previous day they had frisked each person and turned the premises and everyone's room upside down in search of the gun that killed the doctor, to no avail. Now the officers were in the process of questioning all the suspects again. The classes and exercise programs were cancelled for the day, and everyone was asked to stay put until summoned to the administrative office for police interrogation.

Huber spent the morning in her suite engaged in concentrated brainwork. Finally, she formed a plan of action and then phoned Andi, inviting her to the suite. When the young woman learned what Huber had been mulling over and the conclusions she had arrived at, she was flabbergasted at her employer's revelation but had to admit that it all made sense. Then the elder told her of the steps she was about to take.

Andi listened carefully to the game plan and then said, "Now I know why you took me to the putting green yesterday and had me show you exactly where Mr. Camden lay dead." Then she asked, "You're letting me come along, right?"

"Sorry! I've got to do this on my own. Your joining in would make the killer suspicious and my attempt at provocation could fail."

"But it's too dangerous alone; the person's got your piece!" Andi protested.

Huber replied, "Remember, the police searched for it in every corner of the house and grounds. The murderer must have an excellent hiding place for the pistol. My guess is that it's buried somewhere in the woods, and I won't give our culprit time to get to it."

Still edgy, Andi said, "I don't like it, but you're the boss!"

"That's the spirit."

"When are you going to lay your trap?"

"Right after lunch. I'll take my phone along. If you don't see or hear from me half an hour later, alert the sheriff."

Chapter 65

R. A. Huber arrived first and went inside the shed. Emerging equipped with a golf ball and putter, she stationed herself at the edge of the green. She did not have to wait long; in a minute or two she heard the sound of footsteps and turned to meet her quarry.

She said, "Thanks for coming so promptly."

Slightly out of breath, the newcomer asked, "So what did you find here and wanted to show me?" And glancing at the putter, "Surely not this club?"

Huber replied, "I'm puzzled about something and don't want to ask Mrs. Camden directly. Maybe you can enlighten me," and led the way to the third practice hole.

Stopping a few feet away from it, she pointed to the ground and said, "Jeffrey Camden was laying right here after he was struck down, so - -"

Interrupting and motioning to the area near hole number five, the other stated, "You're mistaken. He was over - -" and, realizing the blunder, stopped in mid-sentence.

"That's interesting, Mrs. Demitris! So you know the exact spot where he was murdered?"

The principal stammered, "Eh - - Dr. Ronnquist showed me where he'd found the body."

"You can stop the pretense. I know the truth."

"I have no idea what you mean."

"I'll spell it out for you, then. You cleverly tried to frame Mrs. Camden for the murders and it almost worked. I believe the police are gathering enough evidence against her for an arrest even as we speak. You almost had me fooled as well. She was my main suspect until a couple of days ago."

"You're crazy! Why would I do that? Iris is my friend."

"I'm sure she was at one time, but you've grown to hate her."

"Ridiculous! And what possible reason could I have for killing Jeffrey?"

"You never got over him and took this post to be near Mr. Camden, convinced that eventually you would win him back. When you finally had to admit to yourself that he was committed to Iris body and soul and that you could never have him, not even for a fleeting moment's affair, you set your murderous plan into action."

Demitris snarled, "You've got a vivid imagination! Why would I wait seven years to get my revenge? Do you really believe that I'd stick around this long if I didn't love the job?"

Huber looked her straight in the eye and replied, "That is true. You enjoy being principal of the modeling school and you're good at it, but all these years you had hoped to take over and own the place side by side with Mr. Camden."

"Pure speculation; you don't know anything!"

Huber continued, "I saw the momentary fear and shock in your eyes when I questioned you about your relationship with Mr. Camden. Granted, you recovered fast and almost got away with your explanation, but when you said that you had never been angry at Iris Camden, you overdid it. I started to ask myself lots of questions."

"All conjecture on your part!"

"If you had left well enough alone and not insisted that it was Mrs. Camden who asked you on board instead of the other way around, I wouldn't have blinked an eye, but as it stood, you got me thinking."

After a pause she continued, "There must have been something incriminating in the sketch Nancy drew just before the lights went out that evening after dinner. Why else would you have snatched it? Too bad for you that you left the sketch of the lynched dolls in her folder. That drawing gave you away, you know!"

Emma simply stared at her.

Then R.A. Huber explained, "When I scrutinized the artwork and noticed that third Barbie gloating over the hanged couple, I suddenly knew it all!"

Getting no reaction, she went on, "You cleverly used Paula Parsall to spread gossip to incriminate Mrs. Camden."

"Like what?"

"The rumors of her affair with Chad Richmond, Mr. Camden's inheritance and the suggestion that he alone paid the bill for starting Optimum House, to name a few. Using Mrs. Camden's paperweight to strike down Mr. Camden was another attempt to incriminate her further."

Huber had been nonchalantly practicing her putting at holes three and four. Now she made a point of looking up at Mrs. Demitris, saying, "I don't know what knowledge Lupe had which prompted you to silence her, nor can I imagine how you quickly got a hold of crude peanut oil after you overheard the conversation between Andi and Troy referring to Lupe. All I know is that you pushed Lupe into the pool and that you attempted to kill Troy."

As Huber seemingly transferred her attention back to ball, putter and hole, Emma Demitris stated, "So you lured me to the green to trick me, but you haven't got a shred of evidence."

Hoping her shot in the dark would stick, Huber went on, "That's where you're wrong. Dr. Ronnquist came to see me late Wednesday night."

Emma took the bait and said, more to herself, it seemed, "So he didn't believe me and came to you after talking with me. I knew he had doubts, but thought I was safe to wait with taking action until the next morning."

Then, somewhat fearful of Huber yet proud of her clever accomplishments, she confessed, "You have no idea what it was like for me all those years! I married my ex soon after Jeffrey dumped me in an attempt to get over him. It didn't work, and after my divorce, I sought this job. Once established, I tried to get Jeffrey back. Iris had him mesmerized, however, like she had most men. I never stopped my efforts to get close to him, but he avoided me as though I had a contagious decease."

She took a deep breath and continued, "Then I finally got my chance. Just before this school session started, I saw Iris together with Chad Richmond in a Los Angeles restaurant. It was obvious that they were lovers. I first wanted to ruin Iris and win Jeffrey back. As soon as I got a moment alone with him, I told him about Iris's infidelity, but instead of taking solace in my arms, he shouted, 'Don't talk to me about Iris in that way!' I couldn't believe he'd defend her after knowing that she was cheating on him. So I decided right then and there to kill him and have Iris convicted of his murder. What a perfect revenge!"

She burst into a menacing laugh and said, "You guessed right about Paula. That stupid, gossiping woman thought that she was getting information out of me while it was just the opposite; I used her to get my point across!

"As for Lupe, she saw me coming out the door after I had planted the alarm clock on Paula's scale. She didn't say a word, but gave me a look that asked, *what are you doing coming out of a room in the client's wing?* Lupe was by far the smartest of all the domestic staff, and I knew that eventually she would put two and two together. I had already formed the perfect plan to kill Jeffrey, so I couldn't afford to let her live."

Huber asked, "How did you know that she couldn't swim?"

Again there was that evil laugh as she replied, "I was lucky there! One day when Iris was out of town, Lupe came to the administrative office looking for her. Since I was in charge for the day, she voiced her request to be excused from pool duty because she couldn't swim. I assured her that I would give the message to the administrator. After Lupe caught me coming out of Paula's room, I remembered that I had totally forgotten to tell Iris about the maid's request. That was ideal, of course. People would assume that Iris knew that the girl couldn't swim, so by drowning her I implicated Iris in the crimes even more.

"You wanted to know how I got the peanut oil so promptly. Actually, I had it ready, just in case!"

"Really?"

"I was aware that Lupe and Troy had become friends, but of course had no way of knowing if the maid had discussed her suspicion of me with the boy. So after I took care of her, I thought of equipping myself with some peanut product in case I would also have to silence Troy. I decided to add peanut oil to the salad dressing should it become necessary to get rid of him. After doing some research online and learning that in order to cause a severe allergic reaction it would have to be crude and not refined peanut oil, I shopped for it at a natural foods store. So when I walked past the library that day and overheard Andi's remark to Troy about Lupe, I was ready. It was easy to sneak into the kitchen at night and add the stuff to the clients' salad dressing container."

She snarled, "It would have worked like a charm if your little snitch hadn't rushed to Troy's room to get his medication." And she added, "He might be dead in spite of the effort, for all I know. They wouldn't give me any information at the hospital as to how he is doing."

Huber declared, "Troy survived and will be able to tell his story."

Emma shot back, "He may not know anything, after all, and if he does it'll be hearsay and can't harm me."

"Tell me about the killing of Mr. Camden, then."

"I thought you knew it all," was the mocking reply.

"Oh, indeed I do! You walked up behind him and used Mrs. Camden's paperweight for the initial blow and then finished the job by hitting him with his putter. After the first few blows you must have realized that it was over. So what I want to know is, why the extra beatings?"

Mrs. Demitris showed true emotion for the first time since joining Huber on the green and heatedly answered, "When I saw the blood running from the wounds, I worked myself into a frenzy and delivered stroke after stroke thinking, this one is for denying my love, this one is for making me suffer, this one is for ignoring and humiliating me...and the list went on and on with each additional blow. I finally got ahold of myself, wiped my fingerprints off the putter and dropped it a few feet away from his body. Then I gathered the castle paperweight and without another glance at Jeffrey left and walked toward the entrance of the main building. I first went to the administrative office and, after carefully wiping off my prints and the blood, replaced the paperweight on Iris's desk. Then I climbed the stairs to my room, got undressed and went back to bed."

Huber was aware that her adversary had started to enjoy herself by reliving the moment. So she said, "I figured that it played out something like that, but I thought that you had replaced the paperweight later during the time

Mrs. Camden was resting before being questioned by the sheriff."

Then she asked, "Did you look for a gun in my room?"

"No, I just took the opportunity to search it while you were at lunch. I hoped to find notes or a journal which would tell me how your investigation was going. When I found the ammunition but no gun, I remembered seeing you walking around holding onto your purse and was sure that the gun was in your bag."

"So you had already planned to use it on Dr. Ronnquist?"

"Actually, I just liked the idea of taking it away from you," she replied with a smirk. "I thought it might come in handy if you'd ever pose a threat to me. At the time I was unaware that the doctor had seen me fully dressed that morning. He apparently got a glimpse of me in the hallway. When we saw one another later in the morning, I was wearing a robe and this puzzled him. He questioned me about it on the evening before his death. I vowed that he was mistaken and must have seen someone else early that morning. I'm sure that he told you all that when he came to see you later that night."

Huber managed to nod, pokerfaced. Then she said, "I wonder what was in the sketch Nancy drew during my speech in the dining hall? I mean, there must have been something in that drawing to incriminate you, or you wouldn't have gone to the trouble of stealing it."

Emma erupted in her nasty laugh again and replied, "Or rather, what was missing in the drawing! My seat at the round staff members' table was empty."

Huber thought this over and said, "Yes, I understand. Nancy drew that sketch right before the blackout, and your chair was empty because you had stood up and gone to turn off the switches."

"Exactly!"

For the last several minutes R.A. Huber was conscious that Mrs. Demitris had dropped her guard and was getting cockier with her answers. That could only mean one thing. The woman had somehow eluded the police search by keeping the gun and was carrying it now. Only one way to find out and I might as well get it over with, Huber thought.

So gripping the putter a little tighter, she said, "You have something that belongs to me and I want it back."

"You mean this?" Emma asked, and reached under her jacket, pulling out the .25 pistol and cocking it.

Before Huber had time to swing the golf club at her, there was an outcry in a Southern drawl, "Hold it right there!"

Emma swirled around to face Andi, who had emerged from the bushes opposite the green.

Looking at the pen pistol pointed at her, she mockingly asked, "What can you possibly accomplish with your toy gun?"

"Reckon I'm faster and good at it! Betcha by the time you aim yours, I've tickled you proper with mine!"

Huber seized the moment and, swinging the club in a swift motion the way one would use the sand wedge to get the ball out of a trap, delivered a blow to Emma's wrist. The woman cried out in pain as her arm bounced upward while she pulled the trigger, firing a shot into the air.

Andi stepped close and, disarming the principal, said, "Sorry, boss, for disobeying your order. I compromised and left the big piece at home, only packing this little teaser."

Huber laughed heartily, nearly faint with relief. As her heartbeat returned to normal, she picked up her phone and summoned the sheriff.

Chapter 66

One day at the beginning of September, Peter and Regula were treating Andi to fondue bourgignon at *Chez Tante Jeanne.*

As her next small piece of meat cooked in the rechaud-pot at the center of their table, Andi asked, "So what are we celebrating?"

Peter said, "My wife's being patch-free and successfully having stopped smoking is one cause to celebrate and - -"

"Officially initiating Antoinette LeJeune into R.A. Huber's private investigating business as her assistant is another," Regula picked up the trail.

Andi exclaimed, "So my tryout time is over and I'm hired?"

"You sure are!"

The redhead spontaneously jumped up to hug her employer, nearly knocking Huber's fondue fork out of her hand in the process.

Regula said, "Hiring you is the least I can do for having saved my life up in Big Bear Lake!"

Peter interjected, "I thought you were starting school this fall, Andi?"

"Yes, sir, I enrolled in a junior college and plan to do my sleuthing on the side!"

Then she faced Regula again and said, "Getting back to the trouble at Optimum House, how did you get wise to Emma Demitris? I was sure that Mrs. Camden was the murderess."

"Demitris did an excellent framing job, and I suspected Mrs. Camden as well. But then I remembered Gina

Faracelli-Timble's words: 'Iris is level-headed, and if she feels someone is out to get her, it is most likely true.' I tried to imagine who could possibly be 'out to get' Mrs. Camden, but couldn't come up with any reasonable theory. Then, when I saw that drawing of the lynched Barbie and Ken, the truth suddenly dawned on me and all fell into place as I realized Emma Demitris was the culprit."

She continued, "Also, I couldn't find any reason why Mrs. Camden would lie about offering her friend a job. It seemed more likely that Emma was the liar and had a secret purpose in wanting the position."

Andi nodded and then said, "But why do all the crazy stuff like stealing and the pranks first? Why not go straight to murdering Mr. Camden?"

"I think that she wanted to hurt Mrs. Camden emotionally and ruin her business to begin with, and then land her the ultimate blow of having to stand trial and being convicted of murdering her husband. She succeeded with the first part; Mrs. Camden was a shadow of herself the last time I saw her."

"Another thing I don't get. Why did Mr. Camden tell me he avoided Mrs. Demitris because he felt guilty for dumping her? Why didn't he just stick to the truth that she was trying to hit on him?"

"I guess he was too much of a gentleman."

Peter said, "I still can't believe that you didn't know that Andi was backing you up when you instigated that meeting with someone who carried your gun while you were without a proper weapon."

"I had no idea and didn't even know that she had taken a pistol with her to Optimum House. I also didn't expect that Emma was carrying mine, thinking she'd buried it somewhere. I should have realized that she went to get the pistol, using the excuse of needing to fetch a jacket from her room on a relatively warm day."

Andi remarked, "Remember we were all frisked. Do you know how she managed to hide the piece from the police during their search?"

"I was curious about that too. Of course I wasn't present during the questioning, but the sheriff told me that Emma hid my pistol high up on a tree branch after killing Dr. Ronnquist and retrieved it later when the search was over."

After a pause Regula asked, "By the way, where did you hide *your* gun during the search?"

Andi grinned and replied, "Lucky for me that the Stinger pen pistol is small enough to fit into the Harley's exhaust pipe!"

Chuckling, Peter said, "I like your resourcefulness!" Then getting serious he shook his head and considered, "I don't understand where Emma Demitris is coming from. One moment she's trying to seduce Mr. Camden, and the next she's killing him."

Andi said, "Isn't there a saying, 'When a woman is scorned, all hell breaks loose'?"

Husband and wife looked at one another confused, but then Peter laughed and said, "Oh, you must mean, 'Hell hath no fury like a woman scorned!'"

EPILOGUE

Letter from Cyrilla to Andi, dated October12, postmarked New York City:

"Dear Andi,

"Are you in college yet, and have you done any more sleuthing?

"As for me, girl, you can see from the return address that I'm in New York City and guess what, I've got my foot in the door at Fielding and am a full-fledged woman to boot! Life is good for sure!

"Are you ready for this? A Fielding agent contacted me and not the other way around, imagine that! It was soon after the arrest of Mrs. Demitris and the agent asked if I still could come for an interview. (Guess the news about the murders at Optimum House traveled as far as New York.) I said that I'd love to, but could we make it at a later time as I was scheduled for surgery. Girl, I didn't even have to lie; she didn't ask me what kind of operation! She just said that was okay with her and so she made me an appointment in September, after her return from vacation. This gave me ample time to recuperate. My interview with the people at Fielding went well and here I am! I've had a few jobs already and am loving it.

"Let me know if you change your mind about a modeling career. I'll put in a good word for you.

"Love,
Cyrilla."

Letter from Iris to Chad, dated November 5, postmarked Sidney, Australia:

"Dear Chad,

"This is not easy for me, but I do feel that I owe you an explanation.

"I know that you meant well when you tried to stand by me and offered your support to help me deal with all my tragedies. So I apologize for having sent you on your way and out of my life so forcefully. Also, I was overwhelmed by all that had happened and could not bring myself to answer any of your phone messages.

"As you know, Jeffrey's death hit me hard even though I tried desperately to keep from falling apart by putting all the strength left in me into saving Optimum House. When it turned out that Emma, whom I had tremendous trust in and considered my best friend, had betrayed me, I suffered an emotional and physical collapse.

"Now, far away from home, I am taking one day at the time, and although it will be a slow healing process, I expect that someday I will become whole again.

"I am sorry, Chad, but a lasting relationship between us is out of the question. Despite our romance that started on Maui, my true love was and always will be Jeffrey.

"As for the fate of Optimum House, it could have never been the same again, so I put the place up for sale. I've had offers from a hotel chain, an athletic club, from people who want to start a boarding middle-school and even from a nudist society. I have not accepted any as of yet, but tend to favor the school, even though their offer is the lowest.

"With warm regards,

Iris."

R. A. HUBER MYSTERIES BY ALICE ZOGG

The Fall of Optimum House
The Lonesome Autocrat
Tracking Backward
Turn The Joker Around
Reaching Checkmate

Available at www.amazon.com, www.barnesandnoble.com
and other online vendors.